JUDITH BOWEN

Man of Steele

945

Silhouette Romance

Published by Silhouette Books New York

America's Publisher of Contemporary Romance

For J.R.D.—my mate,
my partner, my best friend.

SILHOUETTE BOOKS
300 E. 42nd St., New York, N.Y. 10017

MAN OF STEELE

ISBN: 0-373-08794-2

First Silhouette Books printing May 1991

Books by Judith Bowen

Silhouette Romance

That Man Next Door #732
Man of Steele #794

JUDITH BOWEN

met her husband when they were editing competing newspapers in British Columbia, and they were married in Gibraltar. She has enjoyed raising sheep and children in Fraser Valley and still spins wool, knits, weaves and puts up dozens of jars of preserves and pickles every year. Her interests include reading, regional cookery, volunteer work, gardening and of course, writing romances.

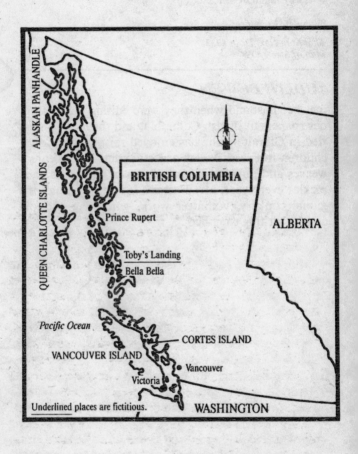

ALASKAN PANHANDLE

QUEEN CHARLOTTE ISLANDS

BRITISH COLUMBIA

Prince Rupert

Toby's Landing

Bella Bella

Pacific Ocean

VANCOUVER ISLAND

CORTES ISLAND

Victoria

Vancouver

ALBERTA

Underlined places are fictitious.

WASHINGTON

Chapter One

"*She!*" It was a bellow of pure outrage. "What do you mean 'she,' Harry? Don't tell me you've fixed me up with a woman?"

The tawny eyes glinted dangerously as the man in the wheelhouse listened to the disembodied squawk from the marine radio. Westbury Island was coming up on the port side and, looming ahead, the snowcapped peaks of the Coast Mountains marked the mainland. The sky was blue—clear, clear blue and, damn it, he should be out there in the sound pulling up salmon.

"When I asked you to round up a deckhand for me, Harry, I wasn't talking about fixing me up with a—with a playmate." A couple of well-chosen curses followed.

Large tanned hands gripped the polished wooden wheel and slowly eased the troller into the main channel. The *Mary Bernice* was forty-two feet long and fifty years old, but everything was in tip-top, gleaming shape and was designed and fitted for operation by one man, the man at the helm: Michael Delano Steele, tall, tanned, shaggy dark hair tumbling well below his collar, unshaven, and—right now—fit to be tied.

"Well, buddy, I guess I'm stuck with her. At least until the springs quit running." He laughed then, at something his friend said, and the smile lines settled easily around his narrowed eyes as he squinted into the distant glare. It made him look more human somehow, a man used to his own company but still a man who worked hard, laughed hard and probably loved hard.

Not that Big Mike Steele had ever been in love; he knew that now. Nor had he any intentions of letting a woman tie him down. That would mean getting a place onshore and giving up his beloved *Mary B*. No woman would put up with the life that he had—away at sea for weeks, sometimes even months at a time. It was a life he loved, a life that he couldn't give up. He'd tried it once, for a woman, and it hadn't worked out—not that he blamed her. But Mike Steele didn't need the same lesson twice.

He grimaced now at the thought of what Harry might have gotten him into for the next couple of weeks. Women! He just didn't need the hassle. Oh, he liked women all right—Harry knew that—but he wanted his women onshore: a little flirtation, a little fun, a night out now and again. Definitely not as crew on the *Mary Bernice* in the richest, busiest fishery of the year. Besides, women aboard were plain bad luck. Every fisherman knew that.

But his usual deckhand, Bob Jeffrey, had come down with acute appendicitis and had had to be airlifted out by the Coast Guard yesterday. He was lucky Harry had been able to round up someone this late in the season and at such short notice.

Oh, well, he thought with a characteristic shrug of his broad shoulders as he reached up to flick off the marine radio, he'd probably been through worse. There was that storm off Cape Rudge where he'd had to jettison his catch and nearly lost the *Mary B,* anyway. And the time he'd been crewing on the Northern Fisheries seiner out of Prince Rupert and had spent three days afloat in a life raft in the icy North Pacific. Having a woman aboard couldn't be much worse than that. Could it?

"Damn it, Harry," he swore softly to himself under his breath, eyes focused on the entrance to the harbor. "I owe you one for this."

Kimberly Bowring sat comfortably on a knoll just up from the tiny harbor at Toby's Landing and shaded her eyes with one slim hand as she scanned the shimmering water. She'd heard the distant drone of big marine diesels and hoped it was the *Mary Bernice.* She'd never met Big Mike Steele, but he was a legend on the north coast, and she hadn't grown up with a father and three brothers—all fishermen—without hearing a few stories about Michael D. Steele. He was the first one out when the season opened, no matter what the weather; he was the first one back with the best catch; and he possessed a seacraft admired by even the most seasoned of his competitors. There hadn't been much he hadn't put the *Mary Bernice* through—or so the stories went.

This was a fine opportunity to crew for the best in the business, Kimberly thought, wishing she felt happier about it. She might even get to see some killer whales, the subject of the thesis she'd put on hold for the summer—maybe forever. Clear blue eyes clouded slightly and she frowned.

In her rush to catch the first available seaplane this morning, she hadn't had time to think over what it would be like crewing for someone other than her father or a brother. Big Mike Steele definitely sounded like the kind of crusty old salt who normally wouldn't have a woman aboard. Not every fisherman was as broad-minded as her father and brothers had been.

Still, she reminded herself, squinting at the bright water, Uncle Harry wouldn't have asked her to sign on if he hadn't been sure. If Harry "Coho" Jenkins said it was okay, that was good enough for Kimberly.

She got to her feet and absently brushed grass from the backside of her faded denims, narrowing her gaze as the troller came into sight, gleaming black hull slicing powerfully through the water at top speed, the boat's registration numbers picked out in white. It was the *Mary Bernice* all right, and it looked like her skipper was in a hurry.

Kimberly shouldered her duffel bag with a quick, practiced heave, feeling a pang as she always did at the sight of the name on the bag: Harvey Bowring, Steveston, British Columbia. Her father and her brother Paul had gone down with their boat in the herring fishery two seasons ago. And nothing—*nothing*—had been the same since.

"I've already talked to Uncle Harry about it," Kimberly'd said when her mother had stared in stony silence at the news that she planned to spend the summer fishing. "He agrees with me. I've got to do it, Ma. You know that. I can't—" a tremor had entered her voice and she'd cleared her throat impatiently "—I can't let this thing get to me. I've got to beat it once and for all."

"Shh, darling. I know." Her mother's words had been softly spoken, her eyes dark with concern. She'd pushed back a wayward lock of Kimberly's hair. "Ach. You're so like your Dad, Kimmie." Her eyes had glistened, but Kimberly could see a gleam of maternal pride twinkling there, too. "All spit and grit, he always said."

Then, last night, when the call had come from Coho Jenkins, her father's longtime friend and almost an uncle to the Bowring children, Kimberly had seen her mother relax for the first time since she'd announced her intentions.

"Oh, Mike Steele, *ja*. You'll be in good hands, Kimmie. He's the very best." And she'd smiled happily, the first happy smile Kimberly could remember seeing in many months. It irritated her, just slightly, that her mother could feel such confidence in a man she had never met, when her own daughter had spent the past week trying to put her fears to rest.

But then, Kimberly thought as she carefully picked her way down the hill toward the government dock, she was up against a living legend, wasn't she? Not flesh and blood like everybody else.

"Wharfinger!"

The wharfinger's sixteen-year-old son ran out of the gray-shingled hut at the end of the government wharf in response to the bellow from aboard the *Mary Bernice* as she slid expertly alongside, her engines throttled down and in reverse.

"Yes, sir!" He caught the lines carelessly tossed from the troller, secured them, then stepped back smartly to drag the fuel hose closer to the *Mary Bernice*'s tanks. So far, it seemed, the man aboard had barely even glanced at the wharf, let alone seen her.

Then why did she get the feeling that he hadn't missed a thing as he moved silently and lithely over the deck with the economy of movement gained from long experience and familiarity with his tasks, checking a gauge here, tugging on a line there? And why did she get the most awful feeling in the pit of her stomach that if this was Mike Steele, this wasn't what she'd been expecting at all?

But it couldn't be. This must be the deckhand she was replacing. She took the opportunity to study him as he reached up to pull on one of the overhead pole lines, muscles shifting in bronzed forearms, his denim shirt rolled back to his elbows. He was tall, an inch or two over six feet she'd guess, and broad, with the well-developed musculature of a man who had spent his life in physical labor.

And he was hairy. Lord, Kimberly thought with a nervous swallow, was he hairy. His hair tumbled down well below the collar of his shirt, dark and thick, and his face was covered with, well, not exactly a beard, more like about five days' growth. His eyebrows were thick and black—she couldn't see his eyes, but somehow she knew they'd be the eyes of an eagle, piercing, direct and full of a fierce light. Kimberly shivered involuntarily. He looked completely untamed, a wild man of the sea.

Thank heaven there was only room for two on a troller, she thought. Imagine sharing close quarters with this man! She was uneasily aware of a prickle at the back of her neck, of a crackle of tension that she knew was part of the instinctive feminine response to the presence of an arresting, superbly male creature. He was that, all right. Even the careless shagginess of his hair and beard set him apart. He was completely, uncompromisingly, his own man, and he clearly didn't give a damn what anyone else might think of him.

She took a deep breath, releasing the unconscious tension that had gripped her for a moment, aware of her relief. There was no question of backing down. She had given her word. If not to Mike Steele, then, more importantly, to Harry who had helped pull the Bowrings through the roughest patch they'd ever been in. No, there was no going back. Besides, she thought, aware of the sudden lump in her throat, she had something she had to prove—to herself.

"Miss Bowring?" His voice was dark, and deep, and surprisingly quiet. He was beside her, and Kimberly blinked. She hadn't noticed him spring lightly from the bow of the troller.

"Oh—I—yes," she said, annoyed at herself for the momentary lapse that had put her immediately, she felt, at a disadvantage. She took the hand he proffered, instantly feeling hard warmth, a callused palm and a steely grip. "I'm Kimberly Bowring. I'm, uh, I'm supposed to meet Mike Steele here. Maybe you know about it," she went on in a rush, her eyes meeting his. She'd been right. He had the eyes of a raptor, hard and cold and fierce. "Is . . . is he aboard?"

"No. He's not," he said, his glance flicking over her shoulder at the *Mary Bernice,* then back at her, his gaze hard, his lips set in a straight, firm line. "I'm Michael Steele."

He still held her hand. Kimberly glanced down for an instant, dismayed, then looked up at his face as he immediately loosened his hand. He took a step back, folded his arms deliberately across his chest, just under the deep V of the open collar of his shirt, and Kimberly's glance lingered for a second or two on silky dark hair curling at the base of his throat. Then, aghast at the image that had flashed, unbidden, through her mind, she raised guilty eyes to his.

"You're...you can't be!" Mike Steele was her Uncle Harry's age, at least she'd always thought so! They were friends and colleagues. This man couldn't be much over thirty! He wasn't the crusty old salt she'd been expecting, a wise old man of the sea who would take her under his wing for the salmon season and help her conquer the fear that had haunted her since the *Gulf Runner* had gone down. She'd explained all that to Uncle Harry; she'd thought he'd understood!

The man in front of her was frowning now, his brow drawn together in a thick black line. "I take it the news doesn't exactly please you, Miss Bowring."

"No!" Then, realizing how rude that must have sounded, she tried to soften her reaction. "It's just that, well, I was expecting someone a little, er, a little older."

"I'm thirty-four," he said flatly, one brow rising sardonically. "Is that old enough? I assure you, my papers are in perfect order."

"No...no. I'm not questioning your abilities, Mr. Steele. It's just that—" She sighed. This wasn't coming out right somehow. "I guess you're not quite what I expected, that's all."

The answer flashed back, soft and dangerous, velvet laced with steel. "Nor are you, Miss Bowring."

"Oh?" She was taken aback for a moment, then, rallying, her eyes met his boldly. "I suppose you were expecting a man."

"No." There was a brief pause. "Harry told me he'd lined up a woman. And I can't do a damn thing about it. Not now. But I'm not exactly thrilled, either." He took a step backward. "Now stand still."

She tensed when she saw that he was looking her over boldly, insolently, like a horse he was considering buying. She saw his tawny eyes, the color of new maple syrup, move slowly over her body, and she flushed, her whole being instantly outraged.

Lazily Mike let his eyes slide from the smooth line of her throat, down across her shoulders, her small, firm breasts, to the curve of her hip and down, down her slender legs to her feet.

Kimberly felt like he'd taken every stitch of clothing off with that one look, and she curled her toes tightly, uncomfortably, in her sneakers. The nerve! Next thing he'd want a look in her mouth, check out her teeth!

"Take off your jacket."

"What—!"

"Your jacket, Miss Bowring. Take it off, please." She was so astonished at his command that she barely registered the faint mockery in his tone as he added the "please." She was even more astonished to find herself obediently shrugging out of her windbreaker, aided unexpectedly by a large hand that shot out and removed it from her shoulders.

"That's better." She thought she saw a golden gleam of humor that was instantly masked as his eyes caught hers briefly before resuming their inspection, this time moving rapidly over her T-shirt and down her body. "Turn around. Please."

This was outrageous! He must be laughing at her—but who could tell? Damned if she'd turn around! "I won't."

"Very well." He shrugged and moved slowly around her, with the sinuous grace she'd already noted. Kimberly knew her cheeks were red and suddenly, childishly, she felt like stamping her foot.

"Are you quite finished with your inspection, Mr. Steele?" She wished the circumstances were a little more suitable to what she hoped was an icily dignified tone.

"Yes."

"You're absolutely sure? Perhaps you'd care to look in my mouth, inspect my molars?" She couldn't help adding sarcastically, "Not that a dental plan would be part of the deckhand employee package, I sup—"

"—Hmm. Now that you mention it . . ."

His teeth flashed white and perfect in his dark face as he grinned suddenly and took a step toward her. Surely he wouldn't really—!

This was too much. Kimberly instinctively stepped backward, loath to have him come near her again. He'd do it, too—he'd have a look at her teeth!

"Miss Bowring . . ." His voice had risen slightly and had a note of concern in it, and he took another quick stride toward her, one hand reaching out. "Watch where you're—"

"Stay away from me, you . . . you—" Kimberly yelled and took another quick step backward, the heel of her sneaker coming up against something hard, and then, before she could regain her balance . . .

"Kimberly!"

She surfaced, gasping with the shock of the cold water, not icy at this time of year, but cold enough. She flicked wet hair out of her eyes, treading water, and sputtered as she swallowed a mouthful.

He was grinning! The wharfinger's son stood beside him, mouth agape, obviously torn between laughing along with Big Mike—so clearly his hero—and rushing over to help her. His mind was made up for him when the fisherman moved toward her himself and squatted down at the edge of the dock, extending a long, tanned arm.

"I'd hoped to prevent that," he said dryly. The gleam of humor in his eyes maddened her. "Here. Grab on." She eyed him, sizing up his position on the wharf. If there was a way she could get him off balance, perhaps grab his hand and then...

"Don't even think about it," he warned, his tawny eyes alight now with laughter and something more. Was it admiration? "So you can swim, too."

"Requirement of the job?"

"It helps."

"I'm just bristling with qualifications, aren't I, Mr. Steele? Despite my misfortune to be born a member of the female sex." She knew her fury was less than impressive as she thrashed about in the water, hair plastered to her head.

"Seems so. Here." She still hadn't taken his hand. Now that she was used to it, the water wasn't half bad. It actually felt refreshing after the long, hot flight up the coast and the long wait on the hillside.

"See this, Sammy, old son?" he said, squinting up at the teenager. "That's a woman for you. Nothing but trouble. Tripping over ropes, sassing you back when they should be paying attention." He shook his head and winked at the teenager. "Take my advice, boy. Keep clear of them as long as you can."

"Don't listen to him, Sammy!" Kimberly shouted from the water. It was hard to sound scathing when her teeth were beginning to chatter from the cold. "What kind of an expert are you, anyway? No woman—" Kimberly sputtered as she swallowed another mouthful of saltwater "—no woman with any...any brain would put up with such a...a prejudiced, arrogant, chauvinistic—''

"Except you, sweetheart." He was grinning now, squatting easily, his jeans tight over strong thighs as he balanced lightly on the balls of his feet. He reminded her of a big cat, lithe, lethal and always ready to spring.

"What's that supposed to mean? And don't you 'sweetheart' me!''

"You're stuck with me, sweetheart," he said, ignoring her fury. "And it looks like I'm stuck with you. At least until I put into port again in a week or two and I can line up somebody else."

"It won't be too soon for me!''

"Good. Just so we don't misunderstand each other." He leaned toward her. "Come on, woman. I haven't got all day.''

She grabbed his hand, strong and warm. Curious to see if she could dislodge him, she tugged, but he was ready for her. With one powerful movement he hoisted her clear of the water and deposited her on the wharf, water streaming out of her hair and clothes. With another rapid movement he peeled off his shirt and carefully wiped her face with it, his own very close now.

She thought, then, with a faint sense of inner hysteria, that nothing in her life had prepared her for this particular moment: the hot sun streaming down, the shiver that racked her as the gooseflesh came up on her body, the ridiculous sense of security and safety she had as this rough-looking giant of a man—this stranger— gently dried her face, the disturbing scent of heated male flesh, so near, so incredibly male.

She closed her eyes to shut out the sight of him, his broad, flat-ribbed chest, muscles moving smoothly under the tanned skin, the silky tangle of hair she'd glimpsed earlier broadening to cover his chest lightly, then tapering down, down, to the belt buckle of his jeans, his eyes, molten now, and dark. A shiver ran through her that had nothing to do with getting soaked.

"Here. Give me that." She snatched his shirt from him with trembling hands and proceeded to rub her face and hair vigorously. She knew she'd sounded ungrateful, but right now she didn't much care.

"Bring us a towel, Sammy!" he yelled to the wharfinger's son, startling her. "You'll find a couple in the wheelhouse." Mike turned again, eyes moving silently over her features. She glared at him, trying desperately not to respond to the faint twinkle in his eyes, and sniffed loudly as moisture formed a droplet near her nose.

"Miss Bowring," he said softly, his eyes holding hers. "I've been fishing for twenty years, damn near, and I've never pulled anything out of the water quite like you before."

"You should know." She sniffed again. "You had a pretty good look before I fell in."

"No offense, ma'am." He raised his hand in a mock salute. "I had to make sure you'd be able to pull your weight if I took you on. If you'd been a man, I'd have looked you over just as carefully."

He looked down again, lazily, insolently, and Kimberly was suddenly aware of her T-shirt clinging to her breasts, nipples erect from the cold under the thin fabric. Her jeans outlined her feminine curves like a second skin.

"Like what you see?" she snapped, furious at herself for the hot color that she knew flooded her face and neck. He took his shirt from her nerveless fingers and gently draped it around her shoulders as Sammy came up with the towels. His casual gesture, she knew with a flash of surprised insight, was meant to protect her feelings, her vulnerability in front of a strange man and a teenage boy.

"I have to admit that I do," he murmured so that only she could hear, and she felt a strange stir in her midriff. "Speaking as a man." Her eyes flew to his, but he wasn't mocking her, not this time. Then he went on, his voice louder. "'Course, from a fisherman's point of view, you are a little on the scrawny side. But my friend Harry says you'll do."

"Scrawny!"

"Yeah." He turned to her, one eyebrow raised, and she could see that golden gleam in his eyes again. "I was hoping you'd be filled out a little more. Bigger. More muscle. It's tough work out there, you know, pulling up salmon."

"I know that. I've done it before."

"That's what Harry said. And beggars can't be choosers. Right now, at least until I put into Bella Bella, you need me and I need you." He flashed a quick, narrowed look at her tousled wet hair, her wet shoulders, his brow setting in a faint frown. "But let's get one thing very clear, Miss Bowring, right from the start. Before you come aboard..."

His eyes were remote and hard again, the glimpse of humor she'd seen in him utterly gone. This was a man completely in control of the situation around him.

"Yes?"

"It's been my experience that women and fishing boats don't mix. I've had one or two women aboard before and they've given me nothing but trouble. Just a minute! Let me finish." Kimberly bit back the angry words that had sprung up. "Now, I'm not going to mince words. If you've got any notions about, well, a little romance aboard ship, you can forget it.''

"Romance! You've got to be—"

He held up one hand. "First of all, you're hired on as a deckhand and you'll be expected to give a day's work for a day's pay. You'll be too tired for any, uh, nightlife, shall we say?" he drawled, one eyebrow cocked knowingly, his hand still held up to silence her.

Kimberly thought she would burst with outrage.

"It's a man's job, in my opinion, and you'll be expected to work like a man. I'd like that to be clear.'' He paused. "And secondly—" he glanced down at her, thoughtfully looking over her flushed, even features, blue eyes brilliant with anger, corn-silk hair stuck to her skull "—despite your more, er, obvious attractions, you're not really my type."

She went pale with shock. The sheer, unmitigated gall! What century was this trollerman living in? What did he think she was? Didn't he know there were dozens of women working as deckhands up and down the coast giving a day's work for a day's pay, had been for twenty or thirty years? Some of them even owned their own boats these days.

"Don't worry about *this* deckhand crawling into your bunk, Mr. Michael-God's-gift-to-women-Steele," she managed, her rage held back behind gritted teeth. "Much as this might come as a big shock to your out-size ego, you're not exactly my type either."

"Good." Completely unperturbed, he looked up at the sky with the experienced eye of a man who lived out-of-doors and noted the time and weather. "Nearly four o'clock. I want to be off Smither's Rock by nightfall."

With that, he turned on his heel and took a few steps toward the end of the wharf. She watched in spite of herself, mesmerized by the male beauty of his bare brown back and the peculiarly graceful ambling gait of the seaman on land. When she didn't follow, he half turned, one eyebrow raised. "Coming?"

"I—I'm not sure," she said, avoiding his eye, a sick feeling gripping her middle. Suddenly the implications of spending a couple of weeks aboard a small vessel with this arrogant man hit her. She wasn't sure the *Mary Bernice* was big enough for the two of them. She'd never met anybody who could rile her as he had in—in barely twenty minutes!—until she was practically spitting. Kimberly Bowring had never dealt with people like that, at that kind of primitive level.

Most of all, it upset her that this man had gotten under her skin so easily. He was a splendid male animal, and something deep within her recognized and responded to that overwhelming masculinity. She'd never met a man like Michael Steele—had never wanted to. Her brothers weren't like that, the men she'd met at university and the aquarium weren't like that.

It wasn't too late to change her mind. She could get the wharfinger to radio Sunshine Air and someone could pick her up the next day. She could be back in Vancouver by tomorrow night and chalk this whole humiliating experience up to bad judgment. She could probably even get her job back at the aquarium if she wanted it. Live and learn, that was what her father had always said. You had to learn from your mistakes.

But was this a mistake? He had said he'd only take her on for a week or so until he put into Bella Bella. Perhaps a week at sea was all she needed, all the time it would take for her to find out what she needed to know.

She frowned and bit her bottom lip to still the shivers, an unconscious, strangely vulnerable gesture.

Mike shrugged, his eyes hooded and unreadable. "Well, suit yourself, Miss Bowring." Had he subtly emphasized the "Miss," or had it been her imagination?

"I've fished the whole season alone before. I can do it again. Make up your mind. I'm casting off in five minutes and, frankly—" he shrugged magnificently "—I don't really give a damn whether you're aboard or not." And he continued down the wharf to settle his fuel bill with the wharfinger without another glance behind him.

Chapter Two

That foot and a half of dark water between the weathered timbers of the government wharf and the deck of the *Mary Bernice* was the longest step Kimberly had ever taken. She took a deep breath and left the relative security of the solid earth behind for—what?—for the restlessness of the sea and the frail hope that somewhere out there, somehow, she would finally find the peace she needed?

"Coming?" Mike asked when he returned from the wharfinger's office and picked up her canvas bag. He waited, one eyebrow raised in a quizzical gesture she was beginning to recognize. For a split second all eternity stopped as their eyes locked helplessly, tawny gold and cloudy blue, and each took measure of the other. As quickly, each looked away. Then, infinitesimally, Kimberly nodded. With one swift motion Mike threw her bag onto the deck and leaped aboard after it, turn-

ing almost as an afterthought to extend a hand to help
her. It had been that easy.

"Your bunk's on the port side, Bowring" was all
Mike had said, gesturing to the hatch leading down to
the cabin, seemingly preoccupied, as though his
thoughts had already turned to other, more important
matters.

A few seconds later Kimberly felt the deep vibrations and heard the rumble of the marine diesels firing
and, slowly, the troller eased away from the wharf.
Sighing once, then shivering as the air moved over her
wet clothing, she tossed her bag below and climbed
down after it.

Everything about the *Mary Bernice*'s living quarters
was small. The neatly designed and outfitted galley was
spotless and gleaming, all the dishes washed up and put
in their places behind rails that would prevent them
from toppling out with the motion of the sea. What did
you expect? Kimberly asked herself wryly. A slob? Of
course not. People who lived in cramped spaces
couldn't afford to be untidy.

Along the sides were varnished wooden lockers for
stowing rain gear, clothing and the rubberized overalls
worn when handling the fish. She looked around her
with grudging admiration, then threw her bag onto the
narrow bunk on the left, noting the starboard bunk,
much larger than hers, which was neatly covered with a
soft duvet and had a built-in bookcase at the head
crammed full of well-worn volumes. What sort of
books did Mike Steele read? She deliberately turned her
back, very aware of the narrowness of the aisle separating her sleeping quarters from his.

There was no plastic here, no concession to the easy
upkeep of twentieth-century materials. The *Mary Ber-*

nice was a spit-and-polish, brass-and-mahogany homage to an older, more relaxed style of fishing. To a time when the almighty dollar didn't rule the fishery and drive men to push themselves and their boats to take chances, when a man took the time and had the inclination to spend the off-season making the endless loving repairs Kimberly knew were essential to keeping up a boat like this.

Funny, she thought, her brow creased as she hopped from one foot to the other, peeling off her wet jeans and rummaging in her duffel bag for dry clothing, who'd have thought Big Mike Steele, trollerman in constant overdrive as she was beginning to think of him, would have a sentimental streak? You had to be a little sentimental to own an old-timer boat like this these days. Ha, she thought, brightening slightly as she pulled a red cotton sweater over her head, maybe the living legend wasn't as rough, tough and gruff as he liked to let on.

"Bowring!"

She grimaced when she heard the bellow from the wheelhouse. So much for that theory! Did the man have to yell all the time?

"Yes?"

"Are you coming up, or shall I come down and give you a hand?"

"I'm on my way!" She scowled as she pulled a brush quickly through her thick, pale hair, still slightly damp, and secured it with an elastic band. Was the offer to help a dig at her supposedly helpless female state? What was the big hurry, anyway?

Jamming her bare feet into a clean pair of sneakers and not bothering to tie them, she clambered up the brass ladder that led to the wheelhouse on the main deck. She moved ahead quietly to stand just behind

Mike's left shoulder. Ignore the wisecracks, she told herself. Don't let him rile you.

"See?" He raised his left arm and pointed off to the left, somewhat ahead of the troller.

There, in the distance, near a small island, Kimberly could just make out some activity in the water. Then it was gone. She moved closer to him automatically, eager to make out what he was pointing at by sighting along his arm. With a quick movement he grabbed her around the shoulders and pulled her tight against his side, bringing up his left hand to hold her chin in the direction he was looking.

"There! Between here and that rocky outcrop. See 'em? Grays." His right hand hadn't left the wheel as the *Mary Bernice* droned toward the fishing grounds, throttle wide open.

His movement had been completely natural, one anyone would have made to help her pinpoint the whale pod. Then why didn't it feel like just anyone?

"What are they doing?" She swallowed, aware of the unusual tightness of her voice.

Mike reached up and brought down a pair of binoculars from an overhead rack and put them to his eyes briefly before handing them to her. "Here. Have a look."

Kimberly lifted the glasses and moved slightly away so that she no longer touched him. She felt like an imposter, her eyes going through the motions of searching out the whale pod while her whole body still felt the imprint of his hard, lean frame against hers, the heat of his body, the faint sandalwood-and-musk scent of his male skin and the iron strength of his arm around her.

You idiot, she cursed herself, grateful for the bulkiness of the sweater she wore, for she knew that her whole body had been instantly aroused by his nearness, and she didn't want anything to give her away.

"Yes! I see them now." She paused, smiling, her attention focused on the magnificent whales as they sounded and surfaced in almost perfect formation, sending their spume heavenward with each breach. "Oh, aren't they gorgeous!"

"They're moving pretty fast," he said. "Probably just on a migration route, although it's a little offseason for that."

She glanced at him briefly, at his eyes narrowed and golden, then looked at the whales again.

"They travel twice a year along here between California and their summer grounds in the Arctic."

"Mmm. I know. I've seen them in the Strait of Georgia, too. Off Steveston." She had once known quite a lot about California gray whales, she mused, watching the pod move swiftly to the north. She'd almost decided to do her thesis on them before she'd fallen in love with killer whales. But—she hesitated, casting a sidelong glance at him—none of that would interest this man.

She reached up to put the binoculars back on the shelf, and when she turned to him, his eyes were carefully neutral as he looked at her sensible, dry clothes, her thick blond hair cinched back.

"You from Steveston?" he asked, his tone detached and polite.

"Not anymore. I've got an apartment in Vancouver now." She smiled. "But I grew up in Steveston. There and on fishing boats."

"Yeah. Harry told me." There was a pause as Mike checked some engine gauges and slightly readjusted the troller's course. The pause lengthened. Kimberly felt vaguely uncomfortable, although why she should she didn't know. After all, fishermen were notoriously laconic. And this one was no doubt no exception. "Harvey Bowring was your father?"

"Yes." She looked out the open window of the wheelhouse, grateful for the breeze that whipped into her eyes, and could account for the sudden moisture there. "He's dead, though. Two years ago."

"Yeah. I heard about the *Gulf Runner.*"

She whirled around, but he wasn't looking at her. His eyes were fixed on the horizon. But of course he would know; the fishing community was tightly knit. News traveled fast. "I'm sorry about your dad."

"Yes, uh, thanks." She watched, wary as he reached up to take down a pair of sunglasses from an overhead shelf and put them on. How much did he know about the accident? The sun was low now, and long rays gilded the water and danced mercilessly in her eyes.

"Want to talk about it?"

"No!" The refusal burst from her before she had even had time to think about it. But she'd meant it. She didn't want to discuss with this man what had happened to her father and brother, and to herself as a result. The fallout from the accident on the *Gulf Runner* was hers and hers alone to deal with. That was what Dr. Gilling had said. She had to slay her own dragons.

She met his gaze, hers turbulent as conflicting emotions tore through her, his fathomless behind the dark lenses. He shrugged and looked at his watch. "We'll be at Poole's Cove in about an hour. You hungry?"

"Starving!" Kimberly felt almost lighthearted as he dropped the subject. She had nothing to hide, or so she kept telling herself. She just didn't want to confess her deepest fears to someone who was, after all, a virtual stranger.

He grinned at her then, his face relaxing, teeth glinting white and strong in his dark face. If he didn't have all that hair, thought Kimberly with a slight smile in response, he might be half good-looking! Then she blushed as she realized the tenor of her thoughts. Handsome is as handsome does, she reminded herself, and her smile disappeared.

"Much as I hate having a woman aboard," he drawled, as though reading her thoughts and underlining her unwelcome presence aboard the *Mary Bernice,* "I do admit to the possibility of one advantage."

He hesitated, a lazy smile warming his features and dragging that reluctant response deep within her again, a warmth she felt at her very center. "Oh? And what's that? I thought women were nothing but bad news in your book."

"They are—aboard ship." He paused and grinned. "But they can be pretty good cooks all the same. Are you?"

"Is that part of the job, Skipper?" She wasn't sure whether or not she should take offense. No doubt this man thought a woman's rightful place was barefoot and pregnant in the kitchen—onshore. But, on the other hand, deckhands often did take care of the galley duties. It was up to each crew to decide upon a division of labor.

"If you can cook, it is. If you can't, forget it."

"Did your other deckhand cook?"

"He thought he did."

Mike's reply was noncommittal, but Kimberly could see the gleam in his eye. Apparently Bob Jeffrey's culinary skills had left something to be desired.

"How about if I cook tonight and you cook tomorrow night?" That seemed fair to Kimberly. She held her breath slightly as he considered her proposal.

"Then we'll take a vote, right, Miss Lib?" Mike grinned down at her, then added in a stage whisper. "Only I get two votes."

She moved toward the hatch.

"Oh, and Bowring?"

"Yes?" She half turned, one foot on the top rung.

He had a pained expression on his face. "See if you can do something about those laces—" he gestured down at her sneakers "—before you trip over something. Again."

"Aye, aye—sir!" She glared at him, snapped a quick salute, then swung down the hatch.

Mike knew it wouldn't have done her blood pressure any good, either, if she had seen his grin a moment later when she began banging pots and pans around in the galley below.

"Did you find everything you wanted?" Mike asked her when he finally came down into the cabin, sniffing the air appreciatively at the succulent smells of grilling steak and stir-fried vegetables. Suddenly the galley seemed even tinier as his big frame took up precious floor space. "Hey, I think you've got the job already, Bowring." He grinned. "Smells pretty good in here."

"You should wait until you taste it before you jump to conclusions." But she smiled, pleased at the compliment. At least he had to admit she could do something right!

Dinner was a surprisingly civilized affair. Or so Kimberly thought as she sat opposite Mike at the little galley table and watched as he refilled her glass with the

Australian claret she'd discovered in a well-stocked drinks cupboard.

The cupboard, constantly cooled by its position against the wall of the troller, only a couple of inches of iron-hard British Columbia fir separating it from the cold Pacific waters, had been only one revelation as she'd opened and closed doors in the galley, searching for the implements and supplies she'd needed to cook dinner, determined not to ask Mike Steele for any help. She'd discovered a surprisingly sophisticated assortment of wines, brandy and port, not just the usual fishermen's fare of Canadian whiskey and rum.

And there was no shortage of good food, either. The built-in freezer was well stocked with various kinds of meat, poultry and fresh-frozen vegetables. There was plenty of salad makings in the refrigerator portion and a whole bin of lemons and limes in cool storage. And, of course, there would always be fresh salmon available.

"No doubt about it, Bowring," Mike said, as he helped himself to some more of the crisply sautéed vegetables. He raised his glass and winked, tawny eyes glowing gold in the warm rays of the setting sun, visible through one of the many portholes that lined the cabin. "The job's yours. Maybe I should think twice about trading you in at Bella Bella."

"So my cooking beats Bob's?" She smiled, drawn in by the warmth of his smile, despite the tiny pang she felt at his reminder that she'd be leaving the *Mary Bernice* as soon as he could round up a male replacement.

"Did you look through all the cupboards?"

She frowned slightly. "I think so."

"Well. Then you must have come across a few cases of baked beans." A smile tugged at the corners of his firm lips, the lower one full and sensual. Kimberly stared, fascinated in spite of herself. She nodded, her eyes rising to his, wondering.

"That was the extent of Bob's kitchen accomplishments, I'm afraid. Open a can of beans, warm it up, throw a chunk of fish into a frying pan. Salmon and beans. Every meal but the odd one I managed to cook. Except breakfast." He grinned at her. "That was eggs and beans."

She laughed for the first time that day. And for a moment it took Mike aback, arrested him just as he finished the story, and he stared at her, taking in the sudden softness the laughter had brought to her features, too often set in challenge and a sort of grim purpose. Then he chuckled, too, a throaty sound of pure pleasure.

"Trouble was, Bob didn't see what the problem was." He leaned toward her, elbows on the table, in a gesture of confidence. "'Ya like beans?' he asked me. 'Sure I do, Bob,' I'd say. 'An' ya like fish, don't ya?' 'Yes,' I'd say. 'Then what the hell ya complainin' about?'" Kimberly pealed with laughter again, and Mike leaned back. "Got me every time with that," he said in mock chagrin.

The *Mary Bernice* swayed gently at the end of her lines, snugly anchored in the calm waters of the cove and, except for the scream of wheeling seabirds and the occasional clank of a line from the trolling poles, hoisted high, there wasn't a sound in the world other than their voices. It was extraordinarily peaceful, and Kimberly felt herself begin to relax, finally. It had been a hard day, a day fraught with emotion, and she was looking forward to her bunk tonight.

"So." She leaned forward, elbows on the table, suddenly aware of the warmth in Mike's eyes as he looked at her, suddenly uncomfortably aware again of the tug of her response to him as a man. She colored slightly, remembering his plain warning to her back on the government wharf. "I—I suppose we'll be fishing early tomorrow. You want me to pack?" She was referring to the job of gutting and packing the fresh salmon on ice as they came up from the sea, each fish gaffed and hook removed by the trollerman in the pit at the rear of the boat. When fishing alone, a trollerman could steer his boat and fish at the same time, the pit cleverly designed for operation by one person.

"Yeah. I've got a little work to do tonight on the lines, check the leaders, hooks. I'm not using any bait right now. They seem to be going for the lures fine without it."

Kimberly looked at him in surprise. This was the most information she'd ever heard him volunteer before.

As though aware that she knew he was rambling, and wondered about it, Mike abruptly got to his feet and took his dirty dishes to the sink. "I'll wash these up. You probably want to get your things sorted out."

"Never mind. I'll take care of the dishes." She had risen to her feet, too, a little confused by Mike's sudden restlessness. They were standing close together in the tiny galley—too close. Kimberly took a deep breath to steady herself and looked up at him, the slight flush still visible across her cheeks. His eyes were almost angry as they met hers, his eyebrows drawn together in a black line.

"Right." He made a movement to go by her, toward the ladder to the main deck, and their bodies brushed lightly together, hips, knees, her breast against the side of his arm. He moved quickly, then, as though he'd been scalded, and before she knew it he'd swung himself up the hatch and was on the deck, his footsteps echoing loudly on the boards above her head.

Now what was that all about? Kimberly frowned as she squirted detergent into the sink and drew some hot water. She washed up the plates and glasses, then scrubbed at the grill vigorously. It helped to dissipate some of her irritation with Mike Steele and the events of the day, and by the time she'd wiped up the little table and put the dishes away, her brow had cleared again.

Men!

Kimberly wasn't completely inexperienced in the ways of men; that would have been impossible, growing up with three boisterous brothers and being around the docks and canneries most of her life. But she wasn't very experienced, either. Curtis Jamieson, the one serious boyfriend she'd ever had, three years ago when she was twenty-one, had been another sort of man altogether.

They'd met at the university where Kimberly was studying marine biology, and the quiet, bespectacled Jamieson had taken her out so frequently, on study dates, on pleasant dinners out to the curry houses they'd both adored, that, within a few months Kimberly had wondered if she might be in love with him. He'd sworn that he was in love with her, but Kimberly had been too uncertain of her feelings for the relationship to progress beyond study dates and good-night kisses, and gradually they'd drifted apart. There had been relief on both sides, Kimberly knew now, although at the time she'd wondered if she was being ridiculously old-fashioned and had felt hurt when Curtis had stopped calling so often.

But Kimberly had felt little more than a vague relief when he'd finally dropped out of her life altogether and had taken up fieldwork at Bamfield to study a sea lion colony there. Since Curtis, she hadn't even been tempted. Was there something wrong with her? After all, virgins her age weren't exactly in the majority.

"You decent down there?" Mike called down from the wheelhouse.

"Of course I am!"

"Just checking." A moment later Mike's long legs descended from the hatch, then he came totally into view. Again the tiny cabin seemed to shrink in size. It was a sensation she knew she'd have to get used to.

His earlier displeasure seemed to have vanished, but he wasn't the easygoing man she'd glimpsed at the table, either. There was a restlessness about him now, a sense of suppressed energy.

"I'm not used to having modest young women sharing my quarters, so I thought I'd better announce my arrival."

"Oh?" she murmured.

"Well, I'm not. Believe what you will."

His eyes glittered momentarily and, again, Kimberly could sense his ruthless energy, the element in him that reminded her somehow of a predator.

"In fact, it's one of the reasons I object to having women aboard. Too distracting."

"Oh, I'm sure a man of your vast experience can control himself, Mr. Steele," she drawled sarcastically. "Particularly when you're dealing with someone who's—as I think you put it so bluntly—not your type, anyway."

To her surprise, instead of taking her up on her cutting remark, he threw back his head and roared with laughter. "Didn't like that, did you?"

"I don't know if any woman would particularly appreciate a remark like that," she said, then rushed on quickly in case he thought she'd had her feelings hurt. "Although it certainly didn't bother me. As you said, it's best that we understand each other right from the start."

"Yes." He leaned against her bunk, where she was kneeling. When he'd come down, she'd been busy stuffing her belongings into the cubbyholes along the side. His tawny eyes, darker now in the dim evening light, rested on her features. "Hmm. Perhaps I was wrong about that. Perhaps you were, too." He leaned closer, resting his weight on his arms, hands spread on her blanket as he bent toward her. "Maybe we should find out. Hmm?"

She scuttled across the bunk into the farthest corner.

He laughed again, then straightened. "Yes, well, actually, I came down so we could run through the routine before you get settled for the night." He watched as she returned to stowing her things into the cubbies. "What's this?" He pointed at a small cassette recorder on her bunk.

"A tape player."

"You like music? What kind?"

He seemed interested, and Kimberly absently picked up the tape player. Music?

"I—I have a few music tapes, Vivaldi, Grieg, that sort of thing." She turned it over in her hand. She might as well be frank. After all, he was bound to see her using it. "I use it mostly for some...some relaxation tapes I brought along."

"What do you mean? Yoga or something? Pan-pipes?" His tone was frankly skeptical.

"No. Just tapes that help me relax, that's all." She raised her eyes in a challenge to his. The gleam that she knew preceded a light remark died suddenly.

"Oh."

"I play it every night, just before I go to sleep. But I've got an earphone, so you won't be disturbed. Just so you know," she went on determinedly.

"I see."

"Was there . . . was there something you wanted to speak to me about?" She gently reminded him of his reason for coming down.

"Yes." He was staring at her, frowning slightly. Then he moved to the end of the bunk. "You use the lockers on this side—I see you've already got stuff in them. Good. The head's over there—" he pointed to a door "—sink, toilet, shower, the usual. I usually sleep in the nude, but in deference to your presence I'll try to re-member to wear something. But I might forget. Just so you know. We start fishing at five o'clock, so that means breakfast at quarter past four. Got that, Bow-ring?" She nodded, her eyes round. "Any questions?"

"Just one."

"What's that?"

"How come the *Mary Bernice* is such a laid-back boat and you're such a hurry-up guy?" For a moment he looked taken aback, then he grinned, the slow lazy grin that sent Kimberly's pulses fluttering.

"Oh, but I'm not, Miss Kimberly Bowring. I'm a very laid-back kind of guy." He reached up and gently stroked her cheek with one thumb, hard and callused and warm. "You just don't know me very well, that's all."

Kimberly shivered, in spite of herself, at the delicacy of the touch. She moved back, away from his hand.

"Now, I've got one question for you." He held up his hand to stop her interruption. "Fair is fair. You ask me a personal question, I ask you one. And this is mine." He bent low again so that she could feel his hot breath against her face, his voice low and intense. "What the hell are you really doing up here in the back of beyond hiring on as a summer deckhand on a salmon boat? I know very well it's not your usual line of work."

She gulped. "My . . . my Uncle Harry arranged it for me."

"Coho Jenkins is your uncle?!"

"Not actually my uncle. But we've always called him 'uncle.' He's known me ever since I was born. He's—was—a friend of my father's."

Mike stepped back and thrust his fists into the pockets of his jeans. He moved restlessly, aggressively, around the small cabin, and Kimberly could hear him swearing soundly under his breath, with the word *Harry* occasionally distinguishable. Then he whirled suddenly. "You haven't answered my question. Why are you up here?"

"To . . . to work as a deckhand, I told you," she said defiantly, thinking rapidly. Then she brightened. "I need the money to go back to school in the fall." Surely he'd accept that. And she did need the money if she was going to finish her thesis on killer whales.

"Maybe you do. But, damn it, that's not why you're here." He paused for a moment in front of her, rocking slightly back and forth on the balls of his feet, his eyes relentlessly boring into hers. "I suppose you're not going to tell me."

"No, I'm not." She held his gaze, although her heart was pounding so loud that she was sure he could hear it. "It doesn't concern you. It's none of your business."

With another muttered oath and a swift movement he vaulted up the ladder again to the main deck. "You're wrong, Bowring!" he yelled down at her. "Everything that happens on this boat concerns me! Everything that happens on this boat *is* my business!"

Several hours later her private terror stalked her again. And, as always, Kimberly could do nothing to stop it.

The swell of the incoming tide lapped ever so gently against the black hull of the *Mary Bernice,* everything aboard quiet and still except for the occasional indignant ruffle and resettling of a sea gull that had chosen the gently swaying mainmast as a perch for the night. The small cove was silent, the bright stars and full moon lighting all below evenly and dimly.

Kimberly moaned in her sleep once, then moaned again, the sound animal-like and deepening to a soft groan. On the starboard bunk Mike raised his head at once, alert to the unaccustomed sound. Then he dropped to the pillow again, half-turned toward the opposite bunk. He waited.

Again he heard the groan, this time louder, thick with pain. And there was a thumping, a soft, muffled sound that repeated itself in a dull staccato. He threw back the duvet and moved across to the other bunk. Careful to make no sound, he drew back the heavy duck curtains that provided some measure of privacy in the small cabin. Then he sucked in his breath, hard.

Kimberly's hair was spread out across her pillow, silken strands tangled by the writhings of her head as she mutely moved, thumping, from side to side on the white linen, her features twisted with anguish. The deep moan came as she pressed one fist to her mouth, the other to her midriff, pressing, in a futile gesture of comfort. Her nightdress had hiked itself past her knees, and one white thigh gleamed in the starlight, the soft curves of her breast half-exposed. The thin fabric clung to her skin in great patches of perspiration.

"Kimberly!" Mike's voice was low. He didn't want to startle her, but he wanted to awaken her from her nightmare, assure her of... of what? His nearness perhaps? Kimberly whimpered, her face contorted, and began breathing hard, afraid of something only she could see.

"Kimberly!" He spoke louder, his face near hers. But there was no response. Then he touched her face, stroked her cheek with one palm and felt the fever, the terror, the desperation of the nightmare that had her in its grip. Instantly she reached up her hand to cover his, to cradle the back of his hand with her palm.

And slowly, ever so slowly, she seemed to settle. The breathing was less rapid, the anguished writhing stopped and the moans gradually quieted. Until suddenly, with a spasm, her body relaxed and, finally, even her hand fell from his, open and soft. The nightmare, from which she couldn't awaken, had finally left her.

For another long moment—he couldn't have said why—he kept his hand on her cheek, feeling the softness, the smoothness, the gentle curve beneath his browned and hardened palm. Then he drew back and, frowning, gazed at the silvered curves of her slender figure. He reached across and gently drew the blanket over her, drawing it right up to her shoulders. Then, as silently as he'd come, he turned and went back to his own bed.

Chapter Three

The aroma of freshly percolated coffee finally penetrated Kimberly's consciousness, and she opened her eyes to the cold gray dawn, feeling a fleeting sense of claustrophobia as she struggled to remember where she was—obviously on a boat, but not the *Gulf Runner*.

"Damn!" she muttered, and swung her legs over the side of the bunk, as she remembered. "Good going, Kimberly! How to make a great first impression." She grabbed her little travel alarm. It was set all right, for four o'clock, only the alarm button was switched off. She could have sworn she'd checked it the previous night.

There was no sign of Mike, but she could hear some clanking sounds from the deck. He was probably getting ready to head for the fishing grounds. Kimberly quickly wriggled into her jeans and a bulky sweater, then pulled thick cotton socks onto her feet and shoved them into rubber boots.

In the tiny bathroom mirror she looked at herself critically, noting the dark lines under her eyes, the pallor due to the lack of sleep. So far, so good, she thought. She'd had the nightmare, all right, but she had had those ashore, too. So far no panic attacks. With luck, she'd beat this thing and go home in a week or so, with Mike Steele none the wiser.

"Oh!" As she emerged from the bathroom, she was startled by the sight of him at the galley stove, seeming larger than ever in his thick Aran sweater. He was pouring himself another mug of coffee, but he looked up immediately, keen eyes appraising her bedraggled appearance.

"I—I'm sorry, Mike," she began. Oversleeping the first day on the job was no way to improve his opinion of female deckhands. "I must have forgotten to set my alarm."

He took a leisurely sip of his coffee, his eyes never leaving hers. "I turned it off."

"What!"

"You heard me. I turned off your alarm."

He was cradling the hot mug in his hands, seemingly warming them. His legs were set wide, aggressively, his shoulders looking broader than ever in the richly textured fisherman's sweater.

"Why . . . what did you do that for?" Kimberly was truly bewildered. And also a little angry. No wonder she'd overslept!

"I thought you needed your rest, Bowring" was all he said, dropping his glance to his mug as he raised it and took another long swallow. Then he bent to the sink, rinsed the mug and put in on the drying rack. "After all," he continued, slowly straightening and turning to face her again, his stance still challenging, his expression unreadable, "you didn't get much sleep last night." There was a pause. "Did you?"

So he had known! Unsure of just how to phrase her answer, Kimberly moved toward the stove and reached for the coffeepot. But before she could touch it he grabbed her wrist in a lightning-swift move and held it tightly, trapped in his viselike grip.

"What have you got to say, Bowring?"

His tone was quiet but intense. She looked up at him, appeal in her eyes. But his were implacable: hard, gold and very cold. Again she was reminded of a great bird of prey.

"I—I'm sorry if I woke you," she said, attempting to take a light tone. "I do get the . . . the occasional nightmare. Probably just something left over from childhood. After all, everybody has a bad dream now and then." She laughed, although even to her ears it sounded constricted and artificial. "Sorry if I bothered you."

He was still holding her arm, and suddenly she realized that it hurt. She pulled and he released her immediately and stepped back. She reached for a mug in the overhead cupboard. When she'd poured a cup, holding her breath a little in the loaded silence that followed her remark, she leaned against the table and absently rubbed her wrist.

"Kimberly," he said, his voice low with an odd, strained note in it.

She glanced up in surprise. It was the first time she could recall that he'd used her first name.

"I'm sorry." He reached out and touched the inside of her wrist. "I wouldn't . . . I didn't mean to hurt you," he said quietly.

She pulled back, sensitive to the skip of her heart as he stroked her skin lightly. God, she had to get used to the presence of this man! She couldn't jump out of her skin every time he came near her.

"That's not all, is it?" he went on softly, one eyebrow slightly raised. He jammed his hands into his back pockets. "About the nightmares?"

Kimberly shook her head, not looking at him.

"Going to tell me about it?"

She hesitated, then shook her head again, this time meeting his eyes. She felt a faint leap just under her ribs as she saw the momentary tenderness in his gaze, then sudden heat that deepened into something else before it was instantly shuttered. Kimberly shivered and, head down, moved closer to the galley stove. "Have you had breakfast?"

"No." There was a brief hesitation, then he continued in his usual curt manner. "That's your job."

The moment had passed, and Kimberly quickly set about getting breakfast on the table, relieved that he hadn't quizzed her further, and relieved, too, that he knew about the nightmares now. It was one more thing she wouldn't have to guard against him finding out, although she knew he wasn't satisfied with her answer. Wearily she passed the back of her wrist over her eyes. What did it really matter, anyway?

Ever since the accident that had claimed the lives of her father and brother, Kimberly had suffered recurring nightmares, a hideous manifestation of her unconscious that she sometimes remembered in the morning, sometimes forgot. Lately the nightmares had poisoned even her waking life, until she'd finally sought therapy. Dr. Gilling had helped her, but he couldn't cure her.

"You can live with it, Kim, with drugs," he'd said, putting it bluntly to her when the weekly sessions had stopped yielding results, "or you can face it and put it behind you. The choice is yours, lass."

Drugs were out. There was no way Kimberly would ever spend the rest of her life—or however long it took to lay her ghosts to rest—on a drug, regardless of how wonderful modern medicine was, regardless of how negligible the side effects were. Her course was clear— she had to come to grips with the inner horror, and she had to fight it. And that, she hoped, was what she was doing by hiring on the *Mary Bernice*. If she didn't conquer her fears, she was jeopardizing her entire future as a marine biologist.

And so far it was working. She hadn't had one recurrence of the formless terror she'd come to recognize as a panic attack, attacks that had started when she began to plan her fieldwork at Robson Bight to study killer whales. The research meant spending time at sea, perhaps the whole summer season out on a chartered boat. And Kimberly just couldn't face that prospect— not since the *Gulf Runner* had gone down. Not yet.

The *Mary Bernice* was moving steadily toward the Queen Charlotte Sound fishing grounds by the time she had cleared away the dishes and climbed to the wheelhouse. Each fisherman knew the haunts favored by the big spring salmon. Finding them took a combination of modern sonar and age-old intuition, and Mike Steele had his favorite places, too.

Another glorious blue-sky day ahead, Kimberly thought, looking around with a shiver of pleasure. The waves shimmered steel-blue, tinged with pink in the glow of sunrise, and the snowcapped mountains on the coastline were shadowed purple, the sun behind their jagged peaks. There wasn't a sign of another human being around, just her and Mike and the *Mary Bernice* moving slowly across the great open sea in a landscape that hadn't changed—except for the logged-off lower slopes of some of the mountains—in a million years.

The air was cool still, but in a few hours they would shed their sweaters and get down to the hard work of harvesting salmon. Trollermen, the elite of an elite industry, used the most sporting method to catch salmon: hook and line. On a modern boat there were enough poles and lines and hooks, all intricately interconnected, to keep the trollermen busy. During the heaviest salmon runs—like now—most trollermen hired on an extra hand to clean and store the salmon on fresh ice in the hold. They were premium-quality salmon: fresh, clean, undamaged and destined for the gourmet tables of the world.

Kimberly surreptitiously watched Mike as he throttled down and began to prepare the boat for trolling. He was full of that suppressed energy she'd felt in him before, and she knew, just knew, that—right now—he was doing what he loved doing most of all.

"Here." He turned to her and handed over the wheel. "Keep her steady on course—" he gestured to the compass and to the distant horizon briefly "—and I'll go throw over the lines. Watch for deadheads." Deadheads were half-submerged drifting logs that could punch a hole in a boat's hull or snarl the underwater fishing lines hopelessly.

"I will." Kimberly stepped up to the big polished wooden wheel and gripped it. She could feel the smooth, vibrant shudder of the powerful engines and the drag of the water on the hull. She was seized unexpectedly with a sense of the pure excitement of fishing, of the chase, something she hadn't felt for a long, long time.

"Can you handle her all right?" Mike asked, grinning down at her.

She flashed a smile back. It felt good. "Of course I can!"

"I'll warn you—she's never had a woman at the wheel before."

"She'll get used to it. There's a first time for everything," she replied pertly, then impulsively stuck her tongue out at him to let him know she knew he was teasing her.

His eyes flared. "Don't do that." He moved infinitesimally closer to her, still smiling.

"Why not?" She tried to keep her eyes on the horizon, in the direction the troller was moving, but she risked a quick, wary glance at him.

"Because you're right, Bowring. There is a first time for everything. And it might be more than you bargained for," he whispered suddenly, close to her ear, his breath fanning an escaped tendril of hair on her cheek. She could feel the tickle of his short beard brushing her ear. "Maybe more than we both bargained for."

Then he was gone, and a few moments later Kimberly heard the creak of gears and windlasses, the groan of the winches that let down the trolling poles and the splash as leaders and lines hit the water.

The next few days were hectic. Kimberly fell into her bunk each night asleep almost before she hit the pillow, and the nightmares didn't return. Every muscle ached, but she pulled her weight without any complaint, and sometimes, when she brought up a flask of coffee and they drank it companionably in the pit at the back of the boat, both too tired to waste any words,

Kimberly thought she saw a glimmer of admiration in
Mike's eyes. One day, their fourth or fifth, she thought,
although it was hard to remember since day seemed to
blur into night and then, too soon, into another gray
dawn, Mike praised her, and it gave her a glow beyond
anything she'd expected.

"How you holding up, Bowring?" he said, snapping
down his overall straps to leave them dangling below his
waist while he reached up to take the coffee flask from
her. They both wore rubberized overalls, which helped
protect them while handling the catch. But the overalls
were hot, and any opportunity to loosen them was
taken. Underneath, Mike was wearing a tight black T-
shirt, which covered his broad muscular chest and
shoulders like a second skin. Kimberly had stepped out
of her overalls when she went down to the galley to
make lunch.

"Fine." She'd never admit to the ache she felt in
every muscle.

"You look cool enough," he said, biting hungrily
into a ham-and-cheese sandwich she'd brought up.
She'd been wearing cotton shorts under her overalls.
"I'd give anything for a swim right now. How about
you?"

"Sure. Where?"

He laughed. "Take your pick, lady. North, south,
east, west, anywhere you want."

"You mean here?" She looked around her, eyes
shaded by the brim of the straw hat she wore. With her
fair coloring she usually burned to a crisp in the summer sun and had long ago learned to use plenty of sunscreen and wear a hat. "Isn't it awfully cold?"

"Sure. But that's only for the first minute or so." He
finished off his sandwich and reached for another.

"Hey, did I tell you? You're doing a great job, Bowring. Fine deckhand and damn sight better cook than Bob ever was." He winked at her, and despite herself she beamed.

"Well, I'm...I'm glad you're satisfied with my work, Skipper." She tried for a light tone, but she knew her flush of pleasure gave her away.

He leaned back, stretching out his long legs in the pit, and gave her an indecipherable look. It held a measure of appraisal, of approval, and of something else—regret perhaps. "In fact," he said slowly, "you're such a good worker, and such a fine cook that I feel like I ought to revise my general opinion of women deckhands. But I don't think that's possible."

His words sank into Kimberly's consciousness slowly as she stirred the sugar into her coffee and examined her own feelings of unexpected pleasure at Mike's praise, offhand though it was. Then, when it did, she looked up at him sharply. "Why not?"

"Because you're still too damn distracting, Bowring." His eyes lazily surveyed her, boldly, without a trace of embarrassment, from her straight nose, just visible under the brim of the hat, to her bare toes.

Kimberly could feel her cheeks flush. And here she thought they'd been getting along so well! He hadn't been baiting her or teasing her as much as he had done the first couple of days. In fact, if anything, he seemed to be avoiding her, staying up on the main deck long after she'd gone to bed. Sometimes she heard the faint wail of his harmonica as he softly played in the darkness and, sad though it often sounded, it comforted, too, and lulled her just before she slept. And then, this morning, she'd awoken to find that he had spent the night in the open air on the main deck. She couldn't blame him—it was balmy and warm at night—but she was still surprised.

"How old are you, Bowring?"

The question startled her. "Twenty-four."

"Ah."

The knowingly raised eyebrows irritated her.

"Got a boyfriend? Or perhaps I should say, a lover?"

"No." She reached out to take the sandwich plate from him, and their fingers accidentally brushed. As always Kimberly's pulse quickened. For some reason she wished she hadn't inadvertently told him there was no man in her life. "But I can't see that it's really any of your business, Mike Steele, whether I have a boyfriend or a lover or not."

"No," he agreed, rising to his full height and looking down at her. "You're right. It's none of my business." He ran one hand through his shaggy hair, then reached down and snapped his overall straps back into position. "But that doesn't stop me from being curious, does it? Those men in Vancouver must be an awful slack bunch."

His tawny golden eyes burned into hers, and Kimberly knew just what he meant. Her cheeks burned red again. Frozen, she couldn't lower her gaze. Mike's eyes moved, once, to her lips, then met hers again, a flicker of annoyance visible, then gone. He frowned slightly and turned away, bending to check the gears on one of the gurdies, the winches that pulled up the stainless-steel fishing lines. Kimberly grabbed the coffee flask and fled.

For a moment she'd thought he'd been going to kiss her! She pressed her hot cheeks with the cool of her palms. And you wanted him to, Kimberly Bowring, you did! I didn't, she argued fiercely with herself, realizing with a dawning sense of dismay that it had been true. She had wanted him to kiss her. He's not your kind of guy, remember? He's . . . he's a chauvinist, a loner. He only wants a woman now and again to warm his bed— onshore, at his convenience.

He's . . . he's a fisherman, for Pete's sake! And you know better than anyone alive never to get mixed up with a fisherman. There's no way—ever—you're going to sit there like your mother, waiting, waiting, wondering if you'll ever see your man again. He's a troller-man, and the sea comes first with trollermen, always will.

Don't forget. You've got one reason for being out here—one. You're here to slay dragons. This is behavioral therapy, my girl, not a singles cruise. You've got a career ahead of you, research, obligations to your family. Sure, maybe there's room for a man in your life someday. But there's no room in your life for a troller-man. Especially this one.

Aghast at the course of her thoughts, Kimberly clambered up the stairs again, pulled on her overalls and gloves and set back to work, head down, afraid even to glance over at the pit where Mike worked silently, pulling gleaming silver salmon from the sea.

That evening, a little earlier than they usually finished for the day, working what was known in the industry as Norwegian shifts—until the fish gave out or a man's strength gave out—Kimberly noticed that Mike had pulled up all the gear when she emerged from the hatchway after washing up the supper dishes. He was about to raise the poles. This usually indicated that they were moving somewhere, but Mike hadn't mentioned it. In fact, they'd barely exchanged a word all afternoon.

"Does this mean we've quit for the day?"

Mike glanced at her and nodded. "It does."

"Where we headed?" The hold was nearly full of salmon now, but there was still room for another day's haul. Suddenly she had a premonition, a sinking feeling. This must mean... "Are you going to Bella Bella?"

"No."

Mike didn't even look at her, absorbed as he was in raising one of the main poles. He looked up, eyes on the lines at the top, and she knew he'd missed the look of relief she was sure had been evident on her face. Then she frowned. Why had the thought of leaving the *Mary Bernice* at Bella Bella tied her stomach into an instant knot? Why wasn't Mike telling her? Well, two could play at this silence game. She crossed her arms and leaned against the wheelhouse.

He seemed to have forgotten she was there, and she watched him, mind wandering for a moment. She caught her breath slightly at the sheer magnificence of his fit male body, sleek muscles shifting and straining under his shirt as he pulled at a recalcitrant line, thighs taut and iron-hard in his faded denims as he braced himself and wrestled with the main pole. The sun gleamed in his dark hair, tumbling down almost past his shoulders. She was used to his shagginess now and barely noticed it, so aware was she of the man underneath.

He turned to her suddenly, caught her gaze, and grinned, his teeth a flash of white in his dark face. He knew she'd been watching him. She looked away with seeming indifference. Then he strode into the wheelhouse, and she followed, standing idly by while he whirled the dials on the marine radio.

"*Ocean Provider. Mary Bernice*—channel 26." He listened, eyes narrowed, to the static-laced reply from the packing boat, the roving vessel that picked up iced salmon from trollers like the *Mary Bernice* at sea, and took it to market. He reached forward and threw the switch that had the big diesels rumbling to life. Then, smoothly, slowly, he swung the troller around and headed obliquely toward the mainland. She might not have existed. "Yeah, roger, Charlie. Headed now for Cinnamon Cove. Should be there in, oh—" he glanced at the sun "—an hour and a half." There was a burst of squawking from the radio. "Roger. See you tomorrow then. Over and out."

Mike replaced the transmitter and turned the radio off. "Got that?" He looked at her briefly, eyes hooded. "We're headed to Cinnamon Cove for tonight. Charlie Makita is going to off-load us tomorrow."

"Then?" She held her breath slightly. She had to hear him say it, that they were going to Bella Bella. And she would be getting off the troller. And she would never see him again. And it wouldn't be a moment too soon. Would it?

"Then? I don't know. We'll see." He turned away indifferently, toward the chart table, and an instant later was lost to her, absorbed in some calculations he was making.

Kimberly wearily climbed back down the companionway, removed her outer clothing and crawled onto her bunk. Oh, this was heaven, just to lie down and nap for an hour or so. She yawned once, then slept in the rumble of the engines and the smooth, rocking motion of the boat through the waves.

When she awoke, she realized it was late, judging by the sun's rays, very low now across the water. She threw back the sheet and headed for the shower. Mike must still be up on the main deck, she thought sleepily, thinking once that she heard a splash. But she didn't see anything moving outside the porthole, just the thick soft green of the cedars and tangled salal growing down to the rocky shoreline. The troller bobbed gently, heavy in the sheltered waters.

The hot water felt good on her aching muscles. She shampooed her hair and rinsed, luxuriously allowing the water to run down her slim body a little longer than she knew she should. Then, briskly, she shut it off and stepped out of the tiny cubicle, reaching for a towel.

She wrapped it around herself and cautiously opened the bathroom door. Where was Mike? She heard some more splashing. It seemed to come from outside. She peeked around the corner. No Mike. Kimberly bent to gather up her shorts and top to stuff into her laundry bag, but then she heard footsteps at the hatchway and whirled to face the ladder. She dropped her clothes, hands instinctively flying to her breast to secure the towel.

"Mike!" Her voice was barely above a whisper as she stared at him, as though at an apparition. Her heart hammered so loudly that she was sure he could hear it in the close confines of the cabin. He'd obviously been for a swim and had come down to rinse off the salt. He was wearing no more than she was, just a white towel draped casually around his hips. His hair was darkened from the water, slicked back, and his skin glistened with droplets. Kimberly dropped her eyes to his chest, unable to meet his burning gaze. But it didn't help. The hairs, silky-looking as she'd remembered from the first days she'd seen him, the day he'd dried her face with his shirt, were tangled and curled, wet, on his tanned chest. She swallowed, hoping to still the pulse she knew was fluttering frantically in her throat. He hadn't moved a muscle, and he hadn't said a word.

"I...the shower's free," she said lamely, and looked up at him again, desperate to restore a veneer of normalcy to the situation. She gestured weakly toward the bathroom door. Sure, Mike Steele had some rough edges and a medieval attitude toward women in general, but so far he had acted the perfect gentleman around her.

Next to staying in the bathroom forever, what she wanted to do most was reach the privacy of her bunk. But that meant she would have to edge past Mike.

He moved slightly to one side. Mesmerized, feeling like a rabbit entranced by a hawk, she moved toward him. Then, one step away, she wrenched her gaze from his and turned to sidle past. Perhaps she was overreacting. After all, they were two adults.

What made her glance at him again, she never knew. Some imp of the perverse. But when she did, she couldn't look away. She saw his jaw, covered with ten days' stubble; his lips, firm and sensual; his nose, straight, with a tiny scar she'd never noticed just over the bridge to one side. She looked at his eyes, saw the lashes, thick and dark. Then she looked into his eyes and was lost, lost in the molten depths, gold and brown and amber, swirling, the eyes of a lion, deep and sultry. Full of pride, full of fierce independence, full of desire. She wasn't touching him. Yet, when she finally dragged her eyes from his, she felt that whatever it was, whatever the keen edge of danger she'd always sensed in this man, it was already too late.

"I...er, excuse me—"

"Excuse you? Lord, woman! You could drive a man crazy!" And he pulled her head around, roughly, and lowered his face to hers, pulling her hard against him with his other arm. She gasped as she felt his skin against hers, only a bit of toweling separating them, then his mouth descended on hers, seeking, searching with a hunger that shocked her in its intensity. Even more shocking was the blaze of sensation that swept along her veins in response. Her first instinct was to pull back, but the hands that were splayed to push against his chest suddenly curled, luxuriating in the satin of his skin beneath her fingers, the crisp hairs, the hammer of his heart beneath her palm. That was instinct, too. And she made a tiny, soft sigh of pleasure, deep in her throat.

At the sound, Mike groaned and his kiss deepened until she thought she would drown in delight, in the fire that swept through her blood, awakening her to sensations she had never known before, never dreamed of knowing. Unabashedly she touched him, felt the hard planes of muscles in his back, moved her hands over his smooth skin, up, until she buried her fingers in the thick wet hair tumbling onto his bare shoulders. His skin was cool from the swim, and his mouth tasted of salt and the sea.

Then, abruptly, Mike pulled back and crushed her to his chest, burying his face in her wet hair. She could hear his heart thudding wildly below her cheek and felt a fine, high exultation sweep through her. He wanted her. This glorious man wanted her, Kimberly Bowring. And she wanted—

Then she paled. What was she thinking? What was happening? This was madness! She stiffened, but he wouldn't release her.

"Mike!"

"Mmm?"

"Let me go! We can't . . . This is crazy!" She tried to pull back, but his arms tightened around her.

"Yes, isn't it?" He raised his head then and looked down at her for a long moment, his eyes alight, glowing.

Then—she could see the transformation almost—his face changed and the tenderness vanished. He suddenly grinned. "What happened, Bowring?" he growled, his voice deep and intimate, but with a mocking note. "That was just supposed to be a kiss. Get rid of a little of the tension that's been flying around lately."

She looked at him, eyes wide with astonishment. What was he saying?

"But I didn't expect us to be so, uh, compatible right off the bat. Did you? Think you could kiss me like that again?"

She pounded her fist against his bare chest. "What do you mean, 'Get rid of tension!' Let go of me!"

He bent down and put his cheek against hers, rubbing it with his stubbly whiskers, a tickly sensation that wasn't altogether unpleasant. Then he put his mouth close to her ear. "Know what I'd like to do now, Bowring? Now that we both understand each other a little better? I'd like to pick you up and put you on my bunk and peel this towel off you slowly and make mad, delicious love to you. All night long." His voice was low, sensual, and it sent tingles down her spine. "Until you fall asleep with my name on your lips and you never have bad dreams again. Until you forget that you ever knew a guy named Paul. What do you say?"

It was like a bucket of icy seawater dashed on her. Paul was her brother! Paul was dead. He thought... So she *must* have cried out during a nightmare....

She twisted and pushed at his bare chest, torn with the need to get away from this man and the way he'd made her feel in his arms, and the fear that if she struggled much harder she might lose her towel, as well.

With a quick movement and a laugh, he evaded her, and before she knew what was happening, his mouth had come down on hers again, this time confident, demanding her surrender. Kimberly stiffened. Then, to her dismay, she felt her body instinctively mold itself to the hard, muscular planes of his, felt her mouth open under his expert onslaught, giving, giving to this man, allowing him access to the deepest, most secret wells in her feminine nature. She felt his kiss change and become infinitely passionate and tender as he responded to her softness and vulnerability.

Finally, when Kimberly thought she'd faint with the sheer sweet pleasure, he lifted his head, almost with regret, and this time his eyes were dark and held a hint of bewilderment. His voice was still low and amused, but with an undercurrent that was utterly serious. "Well? I'm impressed, Miss Bowring. Definitely not a one-off, was it?"

Panting, Kimberly tried to straighten, but he held her trapped, leaning against her, her body against the bunk. "You...you're despicable! You're—" Her eyes glistened with tears at her feelings of helplessness. "Let me go, you arrogant, obnoxious—" She was at a loss for words. "You *caveman!*"

He threw back his head and roared with laughter. "But you've got to admit, Bowring, that the earth moved under our feet, just like they say. Hmm? You know what that means. Don't you?" And he planted soft, delicious kisses along her jawline.

"It means we're on a boat, that's what!" He laughed at her answer and kissed the side of her neck, and every nerve in her body tingled. "Let go of me! To think that for one short deluded minute or two I thought you might be a gentleman!" Still breathing heavily, she glared at him, too aware by far of his nearness, of the heat of his body against hers. "To think that I thought you wouldn't take advantage of me in this sort of situation."

"Advantage?" He grinned at her and dropped his head to place a series of tantalizing kisses along her throat, ending at her earlobe.

She shivered, unable to stop the wave of excitement that swept along her veins.

"Hey, seems to me you wanted it as much as I did, sweetheart. You might seem like the Snow Queen sometimes, all silver and pale and untouchable, but we both know now you're not." He raised his head then and gave her an injured look. "In fact, it seems to me I've been damned polite about keeping my distance until now."

"No! I—"

He stopped her outburst with his mouth again, quickly covering hers, and she pushed hard at his chest, desperately fighting her own treacherous body. How she longed to stop fighting him, to put her arms around him, to cling to him, to let him . . .

"Mike . . ." Her voice was shaky, a bare whisper as he raised his head finally, trailing kisses along her throat again, along her bare shoulder. "Please don't—"

"Caveman, hmm? You think I'm too hairy? Damn!" He grinned and rubbed her nose with the bristly bottom of his chin, and she sputtered with renewed rage.

Then he laughed and suddenly released her. Freed, she moved quickly to gain her bunk, but as she went by he reached over and gave a quick, hard tug at her towel. She shrieked and grabbed at it, whirling on him. But he was already at the bathroom door.

"Oh! How dare you?" She yelled at the closed door, mortified beyond words at what she'd just allowed to happen. Kissing him! That she'd thought, for even a second, that it might have meant something to him—as it had seemed to at first—that he'd regard it as anything more than a rude preliminary to a quick— She shot a venomous glance at the wide bunk across from hers.

"Hey, I'm no gentleman! Remember?" he yelled back with a laugh.

Then she heard the dull roar of the shower. It was obvious what he thought of her, what he wanted from her. She held her hands over her hot cheeks in mortification. He thought that she was just like all the other women deckhands he'd ever known, looking for a little "nightlife" as he called it.

Angrily she dressed and clambered up the ladder, too overwrought to notice the increased pitch of the troller as it tugged at its mooring. There was no way she was going to be there when he came out of the shower. She needed time to cool off. She needed time to think. Tomorrow—no matter what—she would insist he take her to Bella Bella. She had to get off this boat. She knew she couldn't spend another day on the *Mary Bernice*. And—worst of all—she knew it wasn't Mike Steele she was afraid of; it was herself.

She stepped out of the wheelhouse, and her breath was sucked away by a blast of wind. It was nearly dark now, and a sudden flash of lightning in the south lit up the wide north coast sky, jagged forks splitting the blackness with a garish greenish neon, quickly gone. And the thunder followed, thick at first, choked, then with a rapid, deafening staccato that ripped the silence to shreds.

"Oh, my God," Kimberly whispered, her face pale. She put one arm up instinctively, as though to shield herself from something. But there was nothing, not even a drop of rain yet, and the summer storm skirted them well to the south, only the accompanying wind rocking the *Mary Bernice* heavily at anchor, sluggish with her belly full of salmon.

Oh, God! Daddy! Paul! Had she really cried out, or had the words exploded in her brain, as they did at night? She didn't know, knew only that her heart was pounding like a trapped and maddened bird. And her breath was caught in her throat, hot and thick, and her belly crawled with liquid heat, and she wanted to throw up, to die, to get out of here, to move, to stand still, to roll into a tiny ball and hide somewhere, anywhere.

"Kimberly!"

Go away. Leave me alone. Don't see me! Somewhere deep within she begged to be forgotten, to disappear until the attack passed. Knowing it finally would pass never helped. Still, she knew it would. She crawled behind one of the big winches, on the water side, and clenched her arms tightly around her knees, rocking, eyes shut as the terror invaded her guts with its hot, sharp, eager fingers.

"Kimberly! Where are you!" He was standing at the open wheelhouse door. She could tell by the sound. "Damn it, Kimberly, answer me!"

She crouched even lower as she heard his footsteps on the deck and a string of muttered curses under his breath. He was closer now, and he called again, a new note of alarm in his voice. "Kimberly?"

Then he found her. "What the hell are you doing! Why didn't you answer me?" She knew he was standing over her, but she didn't look up, kept her eyes squeezed shut, her knees gripped tightly. *Dear God, make him go away. Make him leave me alone.*

"Kimberly, what's the matter?" Genuine alarm had entered his voice now. "Say something. Are you seasick? What's wrong?" He lowered his voice. Then he reached out and touched her shoulder. "Hey, I'm sorry, I didn't mean to—"

"Leave me alone! Don't touch me!" she screamed, lashing out with her feet and hands in reaction. "Don't... Oh, God!" She covered her face with her hands, and the tears began to roll down her cheeks silently, her anguish dry and aching in her throat. "Oh, God. Daddy...Paul...I'm so sorry. I'm so sorry. I—"

"Kimberly!" He grabbed her again, a hand on each shoulder, and half pulled her to her feet, shaking her. "What are you talking about? I'm Mike—Mike Steele. This isn't the *Gulf Runner.* Your father's dead, Kimberly." He shook her again. "Do you hear me? Dead!"

It was the bluntest, cruelest thing anyone had ever said to her. "I know," she whispered, opening her eyes, staring at him in bewilderment. "I know. And I killed him. It was my fault."

Mike swore vehemently and shook her again.

"I'm...I'm sorry, Daddy, Paul. I—"

"Who the hell's Paul?"

"My brother. He's dead, too. Drowned. I tried, Mike, really I—"

"What are you talking about, Kimberly?" He shook her slightly, and she felt her knees weaken.

"I should have... Maybe if I'd tried harder," she whispered. She closed her eyes in memory. "But it was so cold. I was so cold and—" Her voice broke.

"Kimberly." Mike's voice was hoarse as the full meaning of her words sank in. His fingers tightened on her shoulders. "Kimberly! Don't tell me you were there? You were on the *Gulf Runner* when she went down?"

She opened her eyes then, saw the dawning horror on Mike's face. She nodded, not trusting her voice yet, tears streaming down her pale face. Then she sagged in his grip.

"I... yes... I was... I was the only one who survived."

Chapter Four

Kimberly felt her face crumple as hot tears slid down her cheeks. *Oh, dear God, would this nightmare never end?* For the first time in many months she felt a deep sob rise from her aching throat. Always, before, the fear had silenced her, sent her terror-stricken into some mute solitude of its own creation. Always before, she'd been alone.

Now Kimberly felt the strength of another being enfolding her as Mike pulled her roughly against his chest, his arms strong bands of comfort. She clung to him, her face buried against his shirtfront, sobs racking her slight frame. Through a haze of conflicting emotion she felt rather than heard his soft words of comfort, absorbed his strength and warmth and the gentle stroke of his hand on her hair.

There, before her again, in jagged splinters of vivid memory, was the *Gulf Runner,* capsized in a few moments of wild confusion as the wind howled and shrieked. Mountainous seas had shifted the herring in the overloaded hold in a split second, and from that instant the vessel was doomed. She hadn't seen her father at all, had seen Paul for only a few seconds as he shouted encouragement to her. Then he was swept away in the crash of another wave, and she'd never seen him again, either. Even though she'd looked and looked and the water was so icy cold . . . and . . .

She'd clung to a floating timber—forever it had seemed—battered by the angry waves that broke over her all through that black night until morning when she was found, exhausted, half-drowned. Her rescuers had had to pry her arms away; she'd clung so long and so hard. The bodies of Harvey Bowring and his eldest son had never been found.

She shuddered against Mike's chest, instinctively burrowing deeper into his warmth, squeezing her eyes tightly against the memories. She felt his arms tighten around her, and for a long, long moment out of time she was grateful to lean against him and accept what he offered.

Then she opened her eyes and saw her own hands, as though from a great distance, knuckles white, tightly clenched in the fabric of his shirt, aching with the need to hold on. Her eyes widened as she realized gradually where she was and what had happened.

"Mike?" she whispered, a little dazed. The panic had slowly abated leaving her spent and shaken as it always did, and she gradually realized that she was cradled on Mike Steele's lap in the soft summer darkness, his arms around her, his shirtfront soaked with her tears. They were on the afterdeck of the *Mary Bernice*.

She tried to sit a little straighter and rubbed her eyes vigorously with her sleeve. She looked up at him finally, her eyes huge and brilliant with emotion in the starlight. "I—I'm afraid I've got you all wet. I'm sorry." She smiled tremulously. She couldn't see his expression in the darkness, with his face turned down toward her, his back to the starlit sky.

"Mmm. Yes. So you have."

His words were deep and low, as though he was reluctant to break the silence. He stroked her cheek with the side of his thumb, slowly tracing the last of her tears. Kimberly lowered her eyes, remembering then with a stab of pain their exchange in the cabin earlier.

"Forget it, Kimberly. I've been wet plenty of times before." He hesitated, an odd, husky note in his voice. "But never with a woman's tears."

"Yes. Well." She heard her own voice harden, and she pushed back from his embrace, suddenly afraid of the intimacy of their position. He didn't seem to notice the change in her tone, and instead of letting her go, tightened his arms around her.

"Kimberly..." he began gruffly, then cleared his throat. "I—I had no idea you were on the *Gulf Runner.* I...damn! I didn't even know there were any survivors. If you'd only told me before, I'd have—"

"Look. Forget it, Mike." The last thing she wanted was his pity. "I'm awfully sorry about this and..." She pushed against his chest again, harder this time and he released her suddenly. She staggered a little as they both stood up, the weakness settling in her knees.

"I don't really know what to say." He waved vaguely around the deck in the semidarkness, and she saw him shrug. "Except that I apologize for what happened tonight if it brought this on." He nodded toward the hatchway. "Below. If you're afraid of me, to the point of..." He stopped, then laughed shortly and ran a hand through his shaggy hair. "Well, you don't have to worry. I may not be a gentleman, but you can be sure I wouldn't—"

"It's not that, Mike. You don't have to apologize. Please." She was feeling a little stronger now. Obviously he had no idea of what had really happened to her on the deck. He thought she had suffered some kind of...of hysterical reaction to their embrace in the cabin. Lord! He must think she was a complete child! "It's...it's something else altogether, Mike."

He was silent for a moment. "It's about what happened on the *Gulf Runner,* isn't it? Do you want to talk about it?"

"No." She felt his surprise, felt him stiffen in the darkness at her curt response. "I don't want to discuss it. I—I don't want to think about...what happened tonight. Let's just forget I got kind of, well, upset out here, Mike. Please. It's not your concern."

She staggered as the troller rolled a little in the swell, her legs still weak, and Mike automatically put his arm around her shoulders to steady her. She shook him off, determined to make it back to her bunk on her own, and heard his quick intake of breath.

"I—I don't know what got into me out here, Mike. Really. I—I..." She floundered, trying to gloss over what had happened, conscious of the brittleness of her words in Mike's continued silence.

She looked up at him then, wondering why he didn't say something, anything, to lighten the tension. After what had happened in the cabin, their kiss... No, it was more than a kiss. Kimberly felt her pale cheeks flood with color as she remembered, and now her breakdown on the deck. She cleared her throat nervously. "I want you to, um, know what I do apprec—"

"Kimberly!"

She looked up, startled at his thunderous tone. Anger was a tight mask across his handsome features, his eyes bleak with an emotion she couldn't fathom.

"Y-yes?"

"So nothing happened. Is that what you're trying to tell me? I didn't kiss you and feel the whole world shift around me like I've never felt with any other woman before and neither did you? You didn't spend the past half hour in my arms, crying like your heart was breaking, like I've never heard a woman cry before. Is that life the way Kimberly Bowring sees it? Snap your fingers and nothing happened? Just like that!" His eyes glittered in the faint light, and Kimberly shivered at the contempt in his voice.

"Well. Let me tell you something, Miss Bowring." His voice had lowered to a dangerous pitch. Kimberly couldn't have spoken if her life had depended on it. "I don't live that way and I never will. Nor do the people I respect. Why do you think I do what I do? Damn it! How long are you going to live with the mess of deception you've cooked up for yourself?" She shrank back from his palpable anger. "You might try to fool yourself out here, but you can't fool the sea. Out here it's just the wind and the waves and your own two hands. And that, by God, is how men like me survive—alone."

He stood for a minute or so, watching her, his expression hard in the light of the moon that had just risen. Kimberly thought—hoped—he'd finished, but he went on, his voice dangerously soft.

"But this is your game, little girl. You get to make the rules. If that's the way you want to play it, I guess that's the way we'll play it."

He paused and tipped her chin up to him with one hard hand. Then he leaned down, his face harsh with anger. "Just as long as you know I don't believe a damn thing you say." And with that he turned on his heel and headed for the wheelhouse.

When Kimberly followed ten minutes later—it had taken that long for her to regain her composure on the deck—Mike's bunk was dark and quiet, lights out, heavy curtains pulled tightly around and snapped shut. She had never seen him do that before.

Next morning dawned bright and blue, the promise in the soft breeze of another glorious summer day. Kimberly awoke feeling surprisingly lighthearted and refreshed, as she often did after one of her panic attacks, and peered through the porthole beside her bunk.

The water in the little cove shimmered blue and inviting, and suddenly Kimberly needed to stretch her body, to work out the emotional tangles of the night before in long, slow strokes. She needed to get off the troller.

Quietly she dug her swimsuit, a turquoise maillot, out of a cupboard and wriggled into it. She slipped on an oversize T-shirt as a cover up and peeked out her curtains. Mike's bunk was still quiet. She glanced at her little travel alarm. Half past five! For them this was sleeping in, compared to the early mornings when they were fishing.

The water was cold. But after the first gasp, Kimberly felt cleansed and exhilarated by the fresh chill of the clear green water. She swam hard, then paddled near the shore for a while, finally turning lazily onto her back and floating, eyes unfocused, the wide open sky arching above her as she stared far beyond the blue.

Should she stay aboard the *Mary Bernice?* Or should she insist Mike take her to Bella Bella as she'd decided in a fit of rage last night? Last night! Kimberly felt a slight flush on her cheeks as she closed her eyes and moved her arms slowly beside her body. Numbed as her skin was by the cold water, she could still feel the heat of his body against hers as he'd held her in the narrow passageway of the cabin, as he'd kissed her...

Kimberly's eyes flew open. This daydreaming was madness! No matter how damnably attractive she found him—and what woman wouldn't?—it was sheer folly to even think this way.

Especially after last night. After what had happened last night, she knew he despised her. He'd made that very clear. Nor would she explain herself to him. It was none of his business; she'd told him so many times. Kimberly frowned and turned onto her side, stroking smoothly across the cove.

The panic attacks she'd suffered in the past six months had poisoned her life. It was as though her body—and her mind—had suddenly betrayed her. The hard-won control she'd achieved in her life had turned on her and seized her like a terrier with a rat. Merciless. Unexpected. Sickened her with surprise and terror. Dr. Gilling had said facing the fear was the only real cure. Kimberly trod water and shook the droplets of moisture from her face. Dr. Gilling wouldn't approve of her getting off at Bella Bella. That, he would say, would be running away.

But from what? From the panic that was beginning to seep into her life again in the cramped quarters of the *Mary B?* Or from the troller's captain, a man who'd aroused feelings in her she hadn't dreamed she had? Dr. Gilling couldn't have foreseen Mike Steele. She set herself four more hard lengths of the little cove before climbing aboard the troller.

The heavenly aroma of freshly percolated coffee and frying bacon greeted her as she climbed up the ladder on the side of the hull. For a moment she threw her head back, welcoming the warm sun on her face, her pale hair a tangle of wet silver and gold on her back. If only... She sighed and shook her head. If only what?

"Good morning," she greeted coolly as she descended the ladder. Mike was leaning over the small table, arranging cutlery. She'd be polite after last night, show him nothing had changed.

"Ah, good morning." His eyes rapidly swept over her long, pale legs, her T-shirt clinging wetly to the suit underneath it.

He straightened and she wished he hadn't, because now his bare chest was squarely in her line of vision. Faded denim cutoffs, bare feet.

"Sleep well, Bowring?"

So they were back to that. Well, what had she expected? His tone was deliberately light, but Kimberly could feel the mockery underneath. She raised her eyes and met his boldly. "Fine. You?"

"Not so fine," he said softly, his eyes dropping insolently to her breasts, outlined against the damp T-shirt.

Hot color flooded her cheeks, and she was furious that again her body had betrayed her. Did nothing escape this man's notice? "Excuse me, *Captain*—" she emphasized the formal title, seldom used on fishing vessels. "—I'd like to take a shower."

He waved her past with an exaggerated bow. "Captain, did you say? I guess that makes you first mate, doesn't it? Breakfast is served in five minutes."

She glared at the mocking gleam in his eyes and slammed the door shut behind her. Damn the man, anyway! She never knew how he'd react to anything. One minute he was all tenderness and comfort, like last night on the deck, and the next moment he was as lewd and rude and brash as any fisherman could be. Why should she care, anyway? she asked herself, toweling her hair so hard that it hurt. In a week or so she'd be off this boat and, with luck, she'd never see Mike Steele again.

She opened the door, comfortably dressed in a pair of terry shorts and a sleeveless shirt, frowning a little. Why didn't the thought of leaving at Bella Bella give her the satisfaction she craved?

Mike was buttoning an unbleached cotton shirt as she opened the door, and he met her stare with a quick grin. "Dress rules. No nudity in the galley—unless by prior agreement between the captain and the first mate."

Kimberly met his eyes and laughed. No one could make her laugh as easily and quickly as this man did. The tension between them evaporated, and Kimberly suddenly felt an intense stab of something she barely recognized, it was there and gone so soon—sheer, crazy happiness.

Mike waved her to the tiny table and went to get the coffee from the galley stove. She noted absently that he'd abandoned the buttons on his shirt halfway up, and the gleaming skin of his chest, covered lightly with silky curls, seemed even darker, even more masculine against the coarse white cloth. She shook her head, firmly clearing the images—of her, of him, of them to-gether—that had leaped unbidden into her mind.

"Well, what are your plans for the day?" Mike's eyes were on her face, taking in the pale blush of color, the few freckles that hadn't been there a week ago.

"Plans?"

"Yeah. Charlie's meeting us after lunch, so I thought we'd just take it easy today. No fishing."

"Oh." She took a bite of her toast and chewed slowly. When she met his eyes again, she saw they were on her mouth, speculative. She swallowed. "Maybe I'll catch up on some reading. I'm getting behind."

"Behind on what?"

Mike's friendly inquiry as he poured her another cup of coffee opened the floodgates, and Kimberly found herself telling him about her killer whale research and how she had tentative plans for setting up a field study at Robson Bight next summer. He seemed very interested and asked the kind of questions that told Kimberly he knew something about the subject. Of course he would. Killer whales were often seen up and down this coast.

"So you've done most of the initial planning for a research project?"

She nodded.

"And you've got some preliminary funding already lined up?" She nodded again.

His eyes narrowed slightly. "Then why didn't you start on your research this summer?"

Kimberly sputtered on her mouthful of coffee, and he handed her a napkin, his face carefully blank. "I—I'd planned to, actually," she found herself saying, then wildly cast about for something else to say. There was no way she was confiding in Mike about why she was really on the *Mary Bernice*. "I, uh, something else came up. And I thought I'd put the fieldwork off until next year."

"Sure."

His voice was carefully noncommittal, but Kimberly was suddenly wary.

"Like being afraid of boats maybe. Or the sea. Or maybe it's just men that—"

"No, damn you!" Kimberly leaped to her feet and glared at him. He seemed totally unperturbed as he lifted his mug, one eyebrow raised at her reaction. "If I was afraid of boats, I wouldn't be on this one, would I?"

"I don't know, Bowring. You tell me." He lowered his cup, his eyes holding hers. "You've got all the answers. I've just got a few questions."

"A few questions!" She threw her napkin onto the table, grabbed her dishes and marched over to the sink. Anything to release the sudden burst of rage she felt! Not that *he* seemed to care. "You're prying into what's none of your damn business! And I wish you'd drop the whole subject. If I wanted to tell you all my deep, dark secrets—not that I have any—I would. And I don't!"

"That's fine. No rush. There's plenty of time."

"And that's another thing!" She swung around to face him, hands on her hips. Her mind was made up. "I want you to take me to Bella Bella as soon as Charlie takes the salmon off. I want off this boat as soon as possible. I want—"

"Why?"

"Because you've made it perfectly plain that you don't want me aboard. You didn't want me in the first place. And you said you'd get rid of me as soon as you could and...and... Now I've made up my mind, too. I want off this boat. After last night—" she turned back to the sink, but threw him a quick, accusing glance over her shoulder "—I didn't think I should have to say why," she finished stiffly. She whirled around, astonished, as she heard his burst of laughter.

"After last night?"

She blushed fiercely at his mocking tone, his lazy survey of her body from head to toes, his eyebrow raised skeptically.

"What happened last night, Bowring? Damn! Did I miss something?"

He laughed again and swung himself lithely up the ladder. It wasn't until later that Kimberly realized he hadn't promised to take her to Bella Bella.

Kimberly was dozing on a chaise longue a few hours later, her book abandoned beside her on the deck, as the *Mary Bernice* made its way slowly and steadily toward the area where Mike was to meet Charlie Makita, captain of the *Ocean Provider*. The smooth vibrations of the boat and the clear, gentle heat of the sun on her back had lulled her into half sleep. It was a beautiful day, she was relaxed and content and Mike Steele was at the helm. In her dreamy state all was right with the world.... She barely registered the altered decibel level that indicated a change in the troller's speed.

"Big Mike! How the hell are you?" Kimberly vaguely heard the shout of a male voice as the troller slowed and its engines shut down altogether. In the soft swish of the wash around the boat, she heard the steady rumble of another boat's engine idling. Muzzily she raised her head, blinking in the bright light.

"Not bad, Charlie. Jim." Mike had emerged from the wheelhouse, still clad in only his cutoff denims, to toss a line from the *Mary B* to the packer. "Ready to unload, boys?"

"How's Bob? I heard a chopper had to lift him off a while back. Tough luck, eh?"

"Yeah. He's fine now. I talked to Coho a couple of days ago. Says Bob's doing all right. Won't be back before the end of the season, though."

Coho! That was Harry Jenkins, her uncle—or nearly her uncle. Mike hadn't mentioned he'd talked to him.

"So. Fishin' alone, Mike?" The men hadn't spotted her, lying as she was on the far side of the deck near the wheelhouse.

"Nope. Harry set me up with a replacement."

There was a pause, then Kimberly heard a long, low whistle. "Hey! Is that your—"

Mike cut him off sharply. "Let's get these fish off, Charlie. Jimmy, pull her in tight there." He threw another line to the deckhand on the packer.

Kimberly got up and gathered together her books and sunglasses. She walked over to Mike. "I'll help. Just give me a few minutes to change."

His eyes flashed down her long bare legs under the brief terry shorts, her bare feet. "Never mind, Bowring. Jim'll help."

"But I want to help, Mike," she protested, ignoring the speculative looks of the other two, their frank interest in the conversation. "It's part of my job."

"Damn it, Kimberly," he growled under his breath, his eyebrows coming together in an angry black line. He glanced at the other two swiftly, then back at her, turning his big body so that he stood between her and the two men on the packer. "We don't need your help. Just go...go change."

Kimberly studied him for a moment, deliberately calm. He was embarrassed! He didn't want her standing there like that in a perfectly decent pair of shorts and top being ogled by a couple of his colleagues. "Nevertheless," she finally said quietly so that they wouldn't hear, "it's my job and I'm going to help."

He stared at her a long moment, tawny eyes glaring into her equally determined blue ones. "Suit yourself, Bowring," he said finally under his breath between gritted teeth. Then, louder, he yelled, "Here, Jim, give me a hand with the port hold!" And he swung away from her to help Jim wrestle with the door that was sticking.

Below, Kimberly peeled off her shorts with trembling fingers and pulled on some jeans. What had gotten into Mike! Upstairs she could hear the men's voices as they started moving the salmon from the *Mary B*'s hold to the larger refrigerated one of the packer boat.

"Good-looking deckhand you got there, Mike."

"She's all right." His terse answer didn't encourage further conversation.

There was a raucous burst of laughter from the other two. "I'll say she is! I'd take her aboard anyday. You lucky dog, Mike!" There was silence. Mike didn't answer. Then Jim went on, a little bolder now. "I'll bet her cookin' beats Bob's anyday."

"Yeah," Charlie joked when Mike didn't answer, "and I'll bet that's not all the little lady's got goin' for her, eh, Mike?"

"I don't know what the hell you two are getting at," Kimberly heard Mike say, and she could hear the dangerous edge to his voice, "but I don't like it. I don't want to hear any more comments about my deckhand from you guys. And she's Miss Bowring to you. Not the little lady. I want to see some respect."

That seemed to shut them up for a while. Kimberly felt her heart pounding and her palms sweating. Hearing Mike defend her had done funny things to her insides. All her life Kimberly had fought tooth and nail for everything she'd ever gotten: just like she was fighting for her peace of mind now from the nightmares and anxiety that haunted her. She'd fought with her parents to let her fish alongside her brothers, she'd fought to convince them to allow her to go to college—no one in her family had ever gone before. She'd fought with her professors to take her research as seriously as the projects of the men in her classes: women are still in the minority in the marine sciences. And now it made her knees feel positively weak to hear Mike take her part, put an abrupt end to the speculations of the other men, the idle speculation that was as much a part of the rough, tough male world of the fisherman as storms at sea and raw whiskey.

Kimberly didn't stay below long to examine the tumultuous emotions that washed through her. She wanted to get up there and show the packer and his helper that she could pitch fish just as well as any deckhand. She scrambled up the ladder and put on her rubber overalls in the wheelhouse. When she emerged, she looked as much a fisherman as any of them.

Well, almost. Her tangled skein of pale hair was caught back loosely so that some fell forward over her flushed face. Mike's eyes narrowed when he caught sight of her. No, she'd definitely never be one of the boys.

"Miss Bowring?" He made the introductions, surprising her with his formality and impaling each man with a hard, cold stare as he did so.

They grinned sheepishly and exchanged quick looks of amusement with each other. Wait until they got back to port! Looked like Big Mike Steele had gone soft on women! Or maybe—they cast a couple of sharp looks at the slim blonde pitching fish from the port hold—maybe just one particular woman.

Later, when she tried to thank him, to tell him that she'd overheard him and appreciated his support, he cut her off abruptly, his eyes hooded and distant, his jaw tight. The camaraderie of the past few days seemed to have disappeared since last night, and she sighed, feeling an unexpected loss. She'd never understand this man. Still, it would have been nice to spend what was probably her last day aboard in a reasonably friendly spirit.

After supper, a hasty, silent meal, Mike went up to the wheelhouse and fired up the troller's engines. When Kimberly came up after clearing away the dishes, she was surprised to see they were heading north. She looked around at the snowcapped mountains, the distant glare of the Pacific beyond Queen Charlotte Sound. She wasn't absolutely positive of her directions, but she'd have sworn Bella Bella was slightly south, and east, of course.

"Where are we headed?" she asked Mike tentatively. After his earlier brusqueness, she was hesitant about disturbing him. He looked deep in thought, a slight frown on his dark features.

"Tekla Strait."

"But . . . but that's way north! I thought you were going to Bella Bella."

"No." He shifted his weight to the balls of his feet, then back again, an instinctive athlete's movement she'd seen him make before. He didn't look at her.

"No! What do you mean? I thought I was getting off the boat there. You wanted—"

"I changed my mind, Bowring. I'm keeping you aboard."

"Just like that?" She didn't know whether to be annoyed at his highhandedness at not consulting her or dismayed at the sudden flash of relief that swept through her. He wasn't getting rid of her at Bella Bella! The decision had been taken out of her hands. The words pounded through her whole body with the sudden acceleration of her pulse: *he wanted her to stay aboard*. But . . . but she'd made up her mind to get off. Hadn't she? In her heart of hearts she knew then that she hadn't really wanted to go. She didn't dare to ask herself why.

"Yeah. Just like that, Bowring." He gave her a quick sideways glance, then turned his attention back to the horizon.

"May I . . . may I ask why?" Kimberly's question was hesitant, her voice still full of surprise at this new development.

"Sure." He turned to her and gave her a searching look. "We've got some unfinished business, you and me." Then he gave her a slow, easy smile, the smile that always jolted her somewhere deep within. "Besides, you don't really expect me to get rid of the best damn deckhand I've ever had, do you?"

And that was the only explanation he ever offered.

Chapter Five

They were fishing off the Nlatl River, a great salmon river on the mainland opposite Cape Saint James, the southernmost tip of the Queen Charlotte Islands. Kimberly had never been here before, and she was completely awestruck with the majesty of the sea and the sky and the silent green land rising sharply from the tumble of gray rocks on both sides of the river. In the distance the great jagged spine of the Queen Charlotte Islands loomed, home for untold centuries of the noble Haida people, seamen extraordinaire and possessors of one of the most refined and elaborate cultures of any of the world's aboriginal peoples. That was before the white man came, bringing rotgut whiskey, smallpox and the name of their foreign queen, and bringing greed—greed for furs, for gold, for the very land.

Across the strait was the fabled South Moresby Island, current focus of unrest between the Haida who claimed it as their ancestral home and the loggers who

saw beauty only in the lumber of the towering spruce
and yellow cedar. Mike had promised to take her over
there after they'd off-loaded the salmon next time.
Maybe tomorrow.

Kimberly straightened, took off her heavy gloves and
wiped her brow with the back of her hand. Whew! It
was hot. Mike caught her gesture from where he was
gaffing salmon as they came up from the sea and gave
her a quick grin. She smiled back, watching him for a
moment as he bent over the stern, his back bare and
bronzed under the straps of his overalls.

She'd felt almost comfortable with him since they'd
headed north, a rare feeling of ease that—for the moment—she let herself relax and enjoy. For now, they
were drifting in a tentative, unspoken peace. They'd
shifted course somehow, subtly, silently, and neither
knew when or why it had happened.

It had begun the first night they'd anchored, en route
to the new fishing grounds. Kimberly had realized, with
a sudden trickle of panic, that she couldn't sleep in the
close confines of the cabin. After her attack of the night
before, she needed space, cool air, freedom around her.
She wasn't running away, she told herself, bundling up
her blankets and pillow. She just needed to retrench.

"Need a hand with that?" Mike had come down
from the main deck where he'd been readying equipment for the next leg of the trip.

"No. Thanks, anyway," she said hurriedly, giving
him a quick, guilty glance. "I—I'm going to sleep on
the deck tonight. If it's okay with you." She'd added
that because Mike had slept on the deck himself the past
couple of nights. But there was plenty of room up there,
plenty of room for them both.

"Fine with me," he said, and shrugged, dropping the subject.

When he came up a short while later, she was already snugly in her bedroll, breathing deeply of the fresh salt air and listening to the murmur of the waves and the far cry of seabirds, wondering why she hadn't done this long ago. But sleep seemed far away. For one thing, she was very conscious of Mike in his sleeping bag not five feet away, arms crossed behind his head, gazing up into the silent starry sky.

"Kim?" His voice was soft and deep.

"Mmm?"

"Are you awake?"

"Mmm." She turned slightly onto her side so that she could see him better in the ghostly light.

He stretched one long arm up to the heavens. "Look at Cassiopeia up there, clear as anything. Mother of Andromeda. Do you know it?"

She turned onto her back again, trying to trace out the outline of the constellation in the brilliant jumble of stars overhead.

"See? Kind of like a *W?* That's called Cassiopeia's Chair." He dropped his arm and sighed deeply.

"I've never noticed it before," Kimberly said softly. "I only know the North Star and the Big Dipper."

"Orion?"

"No."

He shifted and turned slightly toward her. "And you're the daughter of a fisherman?"

She could hear the smile in his voice. "Dad never talked much about the stars. I guess he used his electronic stuff for navigation." She was finding this idle, sleepy conversation strangely domestic, almost comforting. "Is that why you've been sleeping out on the deck lately? To study the stars?"

He gave her a curious, penetrating look, then turned back. "No." He sighed again. "All fishermen know the stars, Kimberly. Even if they never mention them." Then he'd rolled over onto his side, away from her, and a few minutes later Kimberly had heard the deep, even breathing that indicated sleep.

They'd fallen into a pleasant routine. While Kimberly prepared a late meal after they'd finished for the day, Mike would hose down and clean up the deck. They were tired again from the heavy work of fishing, eager to sleep at the end of the day and too tuned to the rhythms of the boat and the waves and the steady monotonous work of gaffing, cleaning and packing salmon to want to talk much. But at night, before they slept— and Mike hadn't touched her since the night of her panic attack, not even accidentally—they talked. That was where Kimberly had learned the little she knew about the complicated man who was her boss.

Now she straightened again and threw down her gloves. Her back ached. "I'll go down and make a pot of coffee," she called out, and Mike looked up long enough to nod his approval. She pulled off the heavy overalls and scrambled down the ladder.

She still didn't know much about him, she thought, frowning as she measured out the coffee. One surprise was in discovering that not only was Mike a skilled astronomer, but he knew poetry, too, and she'd been profoundly moved the night he'd recited a few verses of Wordsworth. His deep voice, low and relaxed, had brushed over like the softest, darkest velvet. "Resolution and Independence." How it summed up the man.

But on the subject of himself, his background, his family, he was silent. All she'd learned was that his father was dead, had died ten years before and that his mother lived in Victoria. He had no brothers or sisters. He either ignored her questions or brushed them off with an impatient gesture. The past seemed to hold little interest for Mike Steele. Like Wordsworth's creature of the moor, he lived for the joy of the present.

She settled down in the pit with Mike, reaching over to hand him a mug of coffee. As many days—and nights—as they'd spent together, she had never quite gotten over the sharp prick of awareness she felt whenever she came near him. Now he was wiping the perspiration off his bare chest with a towel, his overall straps down, his long legs stretched out in the pit.

"I've had about enough of this. How about you?" He stretched over and took the coffee from her. "Thanks."

"You want to pack it in for the day?"

"Yeah." He took a swallow of the coffee, then turned to her, his eyes warm and tawny as they held hers. "Let's ditch these fish this afternoon. I think we could get hold of a packer that's in the area, and then let's just have some fun. Take a few days off. Head for the Charlottes." He raised his eyebrows inquiringly over the mug. "What do you say?"

"I think it's a great idea!" Kimberly sipped her coffee thoughtfully. To be frank, she'd welcome a few days' respite from fish. "But how can you afford it, Mike? The springs are biting pretty good." No fisherman she'd ever known had quit while the fishing was good.

"Ah, hell, Kimberly. Money isn't everything." He grinned at her suddenly, and she felt her heart leap under her ribs. "If a man can't take a few days off when he feels like it, what the hell's he working for himself for?"

Kimberly laughed. Put like that ...

Mike had been right: the Northern Fisheries packer *Melanie's Charm* was a few nautical miles away, and by eight o'clock that evening they'd off-loaded the salmon and were making their plans for the next day. Mike showered and put on a clean pair of jeans and a T-shirt while she put a light supper on the table. By nine o'clock they were sitting opposite each other in the tiny galley, arguing good-naturedly over the plans for the next day as though they'd known each other for years.

"I vote for Lyall Island," Mike was saying. "We'll head there early in the morning, spend the day hiking around, then ... I don't know. How about a picnic ... for a start?" He hesitated, his smile warm.

She heard the lazy flirtation in his voice and gave all her attention to her steak. Despite recent appearances to the contrary, he was still a very dangerous man—to her peace of mind. She shook her head, frowning. She'd be wise to spend as much of the day alone as she could. Mike Steele fishing was hard enough for her to cope with; Mike Steele with time on his hands might be more than she could handle.

"Not for me. I can't quite see myself tramping around all day. I'll catch up on a little sleep and lie around. Read, maybe. Maybe in the afternoon—"

"Okay. A compromise." He grinned. "You read while I head for Lyall Island. We'll aim to get there by midafternoon."

Their strategy decided, Kimberly dragged her bed-roll up onto the deck. She'd been surprised to discover how accommodating Mike could be as she got to know him better. Her first impression had been quite the opposite.

Hey, wait a minute, she thought, remembering how peremptorily he'd decided to keep her on the *Mary B*. When he wants something, he gets it; when it doesn't really matter one way or the other, you get it.

That night Kimberly drifted off to sleep with an indescribable sense of rightness and peace surrounding her. Mike was leaning against the mainmast, occasionally blowing some mournful tune on his harmonica, and the waves were rocking her gently, gently... She hadn't had the nightmare for a long time.

Next morning, after dawdling pleasurably over a late breakfast—Mike was nowhere around—Kimberly climbed up the hatch, armed with plenty of sunscreen, her big straw hat and a handful of academic papers. She stopped in amazement when she opened the wheelhouse door. "What in the world are you doing?"

"Never seen a man shave before?"

"Shave! Is *that* what you're doing?" Mike had raggedly snipped off most of his untidy beard and was preparing to shave the remainder with a safety razor. A thick white lather covered one side of his face, and he was sitting on an overturned bucket, stripped to the waist, peering into a small mirror he'd tied to the mainmast.

"Light's better out here." He gave the mirror his full attention and carefully began scraping at the lather with sure, short strokes as Kimberly watched. Then he bent to rinse the razor off in a basin of water on the deck and turned to her with a smile. "What do you think?"

"High time, I'd say," she said, trying to pretend that the sight of him, half-stripped, hadn't affected her in the least. She proceeded to the other side of the deck, unfolded a wooden chaise and settled down, preparing to enjoying the sunshine while she read.

But she found her attention wandering from the whale data. She watched, fascinated, as he finished shaving, rinsed his face, then turned to her with a grin, wiping off the water and remaining lather with a towel. "Better?"

"Much." Her dry answer didn't begin to reflect her real opinion. He was extremely handsome, Kimberly realized with a sudden tug of feeling. Clean-shaven now, his jaw was strong and lean, with a hint of the stubbornness, the determination that had helped make him the stuff of so many legends. His cheekbones were high, his chin square. The harsh dignity of his face and the fierce raptor's eyes were now all of a piece. And she could see his mouth clearly for the first time. Lips straight and firm, uncompromising, the lower one slightly fuller, hinting at a deep sensuality of character. But it would be passion tempered with harshness. It was the face of a man who belonged to the sea. Kimberly shivered at her fancy and turned her eyes back to her monograph.

There was silence for a few moments and gradually she absorbed some of the sense of the words on the page that her eyes kept tracing and retracing. Then she heard another sound and looked up. "What in the name of heaven are you doing now?"

"What does it look like?" He flashed her a quick grin, teeth a blaze of white in his dark face.

"If I didn't know better, I'd say you were trying to cut your own hair."

"Not trying. Damn well cutting it."

And he was, too. He held the scissors awkwardly in his right hand while he held up locks of his dark, curling hair with his left, then tried to coordinate the action in the mirror. Kimberly laughed. He looked so ridiculously awkward!

"Ever do this before?" He gave her a sheepish grin.

That was probably as close as Mike Steele ever got to asking anyone to help him, she thought, feeling unaccountably pleased. "Here." She took the scissors and stood behind him, her eyes meeting his in the mirror. "Now, what do you want me to do?" She studied his hair, gently lifting it this way and that with her fingers.

He hesitated until she looked at him in the mirror. Too late, she realized the ambiguity of her question. There was a very odd look in the depths of his tawny eyes, a darkness, a curious watchfulness.

"You decide, Delilah. You're the barber."

Kimberly frowned. Maybe this wasn't such a good idea. The sun was hot, and she could smell the faint, warm muskiness of his bare shoulders, mixed in with the hot smell of sun on paint and rope and the sharp salt of the sea. His hair felt silky and thick and clean in her hands, and suddenly all she wanted to do was bury her face in it, inhale his unique scent, cleave to his maleness.

Cleave! Good Lord, Kimberly, what's gotten into you? It was instinct and biology and hormones—and she knew it—but that didn't make it any easier to stand there and desperately pretend that nothing was happening. And yet, nothing was, was it?

"Why, er, why don't you go to a barber?" She wanted him to open his eyes and speak normally to her so that she could get rid of the crazy thoughts that kept tumbling through her head. Right now, with his eyes closed in the sun, he looked like a large, sleek cat, replete with some private satisfaction. Far in the distance she could hear the deep, steady drone of a tug as it pulled its huge boom of logs south to the mills from the lonely mountain slopes off Hecate Strait.

"Can't be bothered. Not when I'm fishing." He opened his eyes and grinned at her in the mirror. "I can be quite civilized, you know, if necessary. Wear a suit, tie, go to a barber, get my shoes shined." He closed his eyes when she smiled. "But not when I'm fishing."

She gave her attention to the job she was doing. Not that it mattered a whole lot, she thought. He didn't seem to give a damn one way or the other. A suit? A tie? It occurred to her again that she knew almost nothing about this man. "I suppose that's why you don't shave, either. Can't be bothered."

"That's right. Less chance of sunburn, too, when you're outside all day." He shifted slightly on the overturned bucket, the muscles of his shoulders moving smoothly under the tanned skin, and she felt her breath catch a little in her throat. "Oh, I usually get around to it eventually. Once every couple of weeks. Unless I'm too busy. Or forget." He caught her eyes again in the mirror and smiled slowly. "Or until some beautiful deckhand I'm trying to impress tells me I look like a caveman."

Kimberly blushed and looked down at the growing pile of dark hair on the deck. It was the first reference he'd made to their encounter in the cabin a week ago. She didn't say anything, wishing at the same time her emotions weren't so transparent.

She caught his interested study of her hot cheeks and quite by accident poked his neck with the scissors. He winced. "Ouch!"

"Oh! Sorry, Mike." She examined the back of his neck; it hadn't punctured the skin. She resisted the absolutely mad impulse she suddenly had to touch her lips to the near-injury. Then she brushed the hair away from his shoulders, thoroughly flustered. "I'm afraid it's...it's sticking to you a bit."

"I'm going for a swim, anyway. It'll come off." He stood up and ran his hand through his hair.

It was a little shorter now, would probably come to just below his collar instead of nearly to his shoulders. But it was as good a job as Kimberly could do—in the circumstances.

"Feels great. Thanks, Delilah," he said, smiling down at her. "I didn't know you were a woman of so many talents."

"You're not exactly the world's most particular client, Samson," she said flippantly, glad of the excuse to lighten the moment with a joke.

"Oh, but I am. I'm very, very particular."

His warm gaze prompted her to skitter back to the chaise longue. In a moment she'd picked up her papers again and smiled to herself, a small satisfied smile, as he cleared away the clippings on the deck and tipped out the basin of water. Then he dived overboard and Kimberly heard his yell of sheer physical high spirits as he surfaced, and she smiled again.

"Over there—" Mike pointed a little north of their approach to Lyall Island "—was once a place called Chicken-Hawk-Town. The great Haida warriors, the Ninstints people, lived there. Among many other towns."

"That's a curious name. I wonder why they called it that?"

"Don't know," Mike said, turning to her and smiling.

He had put the slowly cruising troller on automatic pilot and had come up behind her silently as she stood in the bow of the boat, relishing the sea wind over her face, tangling her hair, marveling at the lush green island they were approaching, tall with giant stands of virgin spruce and cedar. No wonder the conservationists wanted this island—just one among hundreds—preserved from the angry slash of the logger's chain saw.

Kimberly didn't know how long he'd stood behind her, and it made her a little uncomfortable to think he'd been watching her unobserved. As he spoke, he'd moved up to rest his forearms on the rails beside her.

"I'd guess it had something to do with a chicken hawk, though, judging by the names of some of the other towns around here." He grinned.

"Oh?" She pushed back a strand of hair that had whipped across her eyes, then turned to him.

"Yeah. Just north of there was a place called Sawbill Town, and south a few miles is Strait-Town-Where-No-Waves-Come-Ashore."

Kimberly laughed.

"And down on Burnaby Island is a place known as Bad-Talking-Town."

"Bad-Talking-Town!" Kimberly laughed again, delightedly, a clear musical sound that spun like silver wind chimes through his blood.

With a half smile Mike reached over and lifted another strand of pale hair that had blown across her face. He smoothed it between thumb and forefinger slowly, then tucked it behind her ear. She looked away quickly, avoiding his eyes.

"Legend has it that the people who lived there bad-mouthed the Bolkus Island people. And since that's where the Haida people—at least the Ravens—all came from, I guess that sort of talk wasn't appreciated." Mike grinned at her.

She hoped he hadn't guessed at the sudden flutter that had gone through her when he touched her hair. She twisted one foot around the railing and shut her eyes in the sun for a moment, breathing deeply.

"You seem to know quite a lot about it," she said finally. Mike was silent for so long that Kimberly opened her eyes again to look at him and was startled to see an expression of intense melancholy and remoteness on his handsome features. Right now, with his dark hair tumbled about, his fierce golden eyes looking far into the distance, his chest bronzed and bare, she could almost imagine him in the prow of a painted Haida war canoe, leading his people into battle. She shivered.

"Cold?" he asked. His eyes were tawny and warm again, and Kimberly shook her head. Her shiver had had nothing to do with the temperature. He reached around her easily to pull her to him briefly, then, as she tensed, he removed his arm and rested his hand on the rail beside her. She regretted stiffening as he'd touched her—after all it was only a friendly hug, wasn't it? But she couldn't help herself—just plain friendly was about the last thing she was feeling about this man. And it wasn't getting any easier. He seemed not to notice her discomfiture.

"I know a great little cove we can anchor in for the night," he said.

She laughed a bit nervously. "Oh? And what's it called?"

He grinned down at her. "Don't know." His eyes moved slowly over her face, absorbing the brilliance of her blue eyes, the faint flush of her wind-whipped cheeks. "But I think from now on I'll call it Woman-Of-The-Shining-Hair Cove."

Perhaps the pure magic of the place had charmed her—charmed them both. Or perhaps it had been something that had happened on the *Mary Bernice*. But something in her center had subtly shifted, so that when Mike touched her later, she knew what the poet had been talking about when he said that the end of our exploring was to arrive where we started and know the place for the first time. But when the inevitable happened, the name of Eliot wasn't in her mind, nor Little Gidding. She was frightened; she was not ready. But would she ever be?

Mike had laughed and teased her about not wanting to go into the water. She lay on her deck chair, pretending an absorbing interest in her papers, all the while very aware of him striding around the troller half-naked, clad only in a pair of navy swimming trunks. Not the very brief kind, she was pleased to note—she hated the bikini-style she usually saw on Vancouver beaches—but just a standard twill sort, very unprepossessing. Or they would have been on someone else. Someone less arrestingly, superbly masculine. With a supreme effort of will Kimberly kept her eyes resolutely on the page, her expression carefully blank.

"Coming in?" Mike tossed the inflated orange dinghy overboard, then gave her a narrowed glance.

"In? Oh, in a while..." She looked up, making her excuses, shading her eyes with one hand from the brilliant sun. Perhaps that was why she was so taken aback—she hadn't seen his intent.

GOOD NEWS! *You can get up to SIX GIFTS—FREE!*

If offer card is missing, write to: Silhouette Reader Service, 3010 Walden Ave., P.O. Box 1867, Buffalo, NY 14269-1867

▼ DETACH AND MAIL CARD TODAY! ▼

FIND OUT <u>INSTANTLY</u> IF YOU GET
UP TO 6 FREE GIFTS IN THE
Lucky Carnival Wheel

▼ **SCRATCH-OFF GAME!** ▼

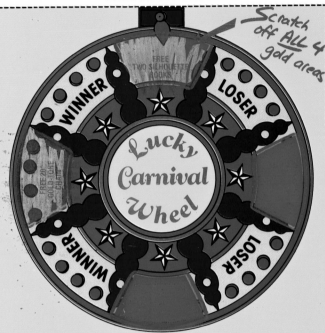

Scratch off <u>ALL 4</u> gold areas

YES! I have scratched off the 4 Gold Areas above. Please send me all the gifts for which I qualify. I understand I am under no obligation to purchase any books, as explained on the opposite page.

215 CIS ACJE
(U-SIL-R-05/91)

NAME

ADDRESS APT.

CITY STATE ZIP

▼ DETACH AND MAIL CARD TODAY! ▼

HOW TO PLAY:

1. With a coin, carefully scratch off the 4 gold areas on your Lucky Carnival Wheel. You could get one or more free Silhouette Romance™ novels, and possibly other gifts, depending on what is revealed beneath the scratch-off areas.

2. Return your Lucky Carnival Wheel game card, and we'll immediately send you the books and gifts you qualify for ABSOLUTELY FREE!

3. Then, unless you tell us otherwise, every month we'll send you 6 additional novels to read and enjoy. You can return them and owe nothing. But if you decide to keep them, you'll pay only $2.25* per book! NO CHARGE FOR DELIVERY! NO HIDDEN EXTRAS!

4. Your satisfaction is always guaranteed and you may cancel at any time just by dropping us a note or by returning any shipment at our cost. Of course, the FREE books and gifts remain yours to keep!

No Cost!
No Risk!
No Obligation to Buy!

PLAY THE

Lucky Carnival Wheel

GAME...

GET AS MANY AS SIX GIFTS FREE!

With one stride Mike was beside her, one large hand relieving her of her book, the other behind her back. In one smooth motion she was in his arms.

"Mike!" He was striding to the side of the boat. "What are you doing? Don't you dare!" In desperation she clutched at his neck and shoulders. He paused.

"So that's what it takes to get you to put your arms around me, Bowring?"

She didn't like the devilish glint in his tawny eyes. Nor the way his eyes moved slowly to her mouth, lingered there, the way he hesitated as though weighing the odds, whether it might be worthwhile to take the time to kiss her.

"Put me down this instant!"

"What have you got under that...that sack?" He peered down at the oversize T-shirt covering her black bikini. Hooking one finger in the neck of the shirt with the hand that held her flailing legs, he looked underneath. "Hmm. You'll do." And with that he took one more step and tossed her over the side of the *Mary Bernice*.

Kimberly came up immediately, gasping and sputtering and yelling all at once just in time to see him slice though the air in a clean dive into the water beside her. "You beast!" She pummeled him as he came up, shaking the hair out of his eyes, spitting out saltwater and grinning a mile wide. "You had no right—" He slammed the heel of his hand down hard on the water, sending spray into her face, and she gasped again. This time she was grinning when she spit out the water. The man was impossible.

"Race you to the dinghy!" she heard as he swam rapidly out of range of her return volley. When she got there, Mike was already aboard the overturned dinghy, and he fended her off, splashing and dunking her whenever she got close. Kimberly was laughing and choking at the same time.

"King of the castle, eh?" she yelled. "We'll see about that!" And she took a deep breath and dived under the dinghy, coming up for air in the pocket under the inflated rubber sides. She could see the deep depression in the center of the overturned bottom of the boat where Mike's big body was. She giggled to herself, treading water, shivering with excitement.

She didn't have long to wait. As soon as Mike edged over to the side to see where she'd gone and why she wasn't coming up, she gave a mighty heave to the far side of the raft and heard a shout as Mike tipped over. With another quick movement, Kimberly got a knee up, and in an instant she was aboard.

Mike met her delighted shriek of laughter with a wide grin. He'd never, ever, seen Kimberly let go like this.

"You asked for it!" With one smooth movement— Kimberly wasn't able to fend him off quite as well as he'd been able to—he spilled her off the side she'd climbed up on then they both struggled to get up on opposite sides of the raft, the poor craft geeing and hawing like a demented rodeo pony. At the same instant they both got a foothold and hauled themselves aboard, falling into the center of the overturned raft together, panting with laughter.

Kimberly's belly ached with the effort. She couldn't remember when she'd had so much fun.

"Now what?" she asked, content for the moment just to try to catch her breath. The sky above was blue, blue, blue. But the clouds bobbed around crazily as the rubber dinghy rode the wavelets. She felt Mike roll toward her. He put one arm across her, resting his hand against the rounded side to stabilize himself.

He was grinning, the water slicking back his hair and shining on his face. His smile lasted until his eyes met hers. Tawny gold met shining blue and held. Then gradually his smile faded until he wasn't smiling anymore. And neither was she.

Kimberly caught her breath, mesmerized by the look in his eyes. The world had vanished. Lyall Island looming not a hundred yards away, a thirty-five-ton salmon troller, the entire Pacific Ocean—all had disappeared. The only world left was within an orange rubber dinghy with a blue bottom. And that was upside down.

"Now what..." He repeated her question very softly, and it wasn't a question any longer. Slowly, infinitely slowly, he brought his hand up to her face, stroked her cheek gently, feather-light, around the curve of her jaw, to her chin. Then he traced her lower lip with his thumb, his eyes intent. Down, down, his hand moved, gently along the line of her throat, starting an involuntary tremor as Kimberly felt the thickness gather in her blood, the deep thud of her heart. Then he touched her breast, his long, lean fingers curving to mold the shape of it lightly, barely brushing the wet cloth of her shirt. She trembled, knowing her response to him was written there plainly. She felt no shame. Right now she was Woman, and he was infinitely desirable Man.

"Now... this," he whispered, answering himself. In wonder she watched as his dark head bent to her breast. He took one aching nipple into his mouth, through the wet cloth of her shirt and bikini top, and she shuddered at the sensation that ripped through her. Reacting blindly, she laced her fingers through his hair, holding

him to her even closer, her body trembling with pleasure as his mouth moved on her breast.

She tried to suppress the strangled little moan she
made as he raised his head, his face wet from her shirt.
His eyes burned into hers.

"This..." he breathed again, almost reverently,
looking down at the soft curves of her mouth, bending
to brush her lips lightly with his. He tried to hold himself in check, until she reached up to him and pulled him
closer. Then, with a groan his mouth came down on
hers, and they were clinging to each other, their mouths
fused and hungry, male and female, exploring the ancient secrets of lips and tongue.

Kimberly wrapped her arms around him, feeling the
hard planes of his bare chest against her breasts, flat-
tening them, feeling the iron-hard muscles of his back
under her palms. A hot tide of need swept through her
so swiftly and so inexorably that she gasped against his
mouth. He groaned and began kissing her face, her
throat, her closed eyelids, her wet hair.

"Oh, Lord, Kimberly," he muttered, his heart thudding wildly against her breast. "You don't know what
you do to me."

"I do," she breathed.

"No, you don't," he said savagely, still under his
breath. He bit her gently at the smooth juncture of neck
and shoulder, and she gasped at the spasm of fiery
pleasure that surged through her veins. "You're a fever inside me, Kimberly. You're in my very blood. I
can't stop thinking about you—I can't! I've never
wanted a woman as much as I want you. Never!" he
said fiercely, taking her mouth again in a deep, sweet
kiss, then moving his body over hers suddenly, his leg
thrusting between her thighs.

At that movement, so graphically demonstrating his desire, Kimberly suddenly stiffened. This wasn't a fantasy! None of it! She wasn't dreaming that she was in Mike Steele's arms, giving him pleasure with her hands and mouth, taking pleasure from his. She really *was* in his arms, the reality more potent, more wildly exciting than she'd ever dared dream. This was happening... really happening. She was holding him, she was kissing him, she was loving him and... And she couldn't let it happen. She couldn't!

With a wild cry Kimberly wrenched herself away from him, rolling to the side.

"What the—?"

She heard Mike's startled exclamation, and then was over the side, welcoming the cold water for the shock it gave her, a shock she desperately needed to bring her back to reality. You fool, she thought, not sure if it was tears or the salt water blinding her as she struck out for the pebbled shore of Lyall Island. You fool, you fool...

"Kimberly, come back!" She heard his shout but she didn't pause. "Damn it, Kimberly! I'm not finished with you."

But I am with you! she thought, her mind in a panic. I have to be—there's no other way. She sliced through the water at top speed, thankful for her strength and fitness, thankful for the stamina she'd built up over years spent near and in the water. She didn't hear Mike. But with only thirty yards to go she risked a quick glance over her shoulder. Then terror gave a burst of speed to her efforts.

He was right behind her, and gaining fast.

Chapter Six

She had just reached the shallows and was wildly trying to run for shore, the water dragging at her knees and thighs when Mike reached her.

"What the hell are you trying to prove, Bowring?" He grabbed her by the shoulders from behind and spun her around. "What is this? Some new seduction technique?" he asked angrily. "Because if it is, I think it could stand a little refinement."

Her eyes flew to his and anger surged in her, too. "Take your hands off me!"

"If I have to, I'd rather lose my breath in bed with a woman, making love, not swimming a hundred yards after a...a tease!" He spit the word out with obvious distaste and his eyes glittered. He was angry, as angry as she'd ever seen him. For a fleeting few seconds Kimberly felt real fear.

"I'm not a tease. I—I just don't want you to touch me." Her anger and fear suddenly burst loose. "Damn it! Can't you get the message? I don't want you! I don't want you to touch me!''

"I get the message all right," he said, his eyes narrowing. "But that's not the message I get." With a single movement he picked her up in his arms and began wading ashore with her.

"Let me go! Quit picking me up all the time. I'm not a child!" She tried to hit him with her fists, but he took no notice of her. He was muttering something angrily under his breath. Where was he taking her? Panic suddenly struck, and with a burst of energy she managed to slip out of his grasp, leaving her oversize wet T-shirt behind. She began to run, a hysterical image of Peter Rabbit losing his blue coat with ten brass buttons in a similar manner flying through her head. She ran like the wind, she knew not where.

But it didn't matter. Mike caught her before she made the mossy hummocks separating the rocky beach from the towering magical forest, even now shrouded with wisps of fog, thick ropes of hanging lichen and tiny brilliant flowers flickering and registering at the edge of her vision.

"Damn it, woman! Listen to me." He spun her around again, his fingers biting into the soft flesh of her shoulders. "What the hell's the matter with you? What are you afraid of? You'd think I was going to rape you or something!"

She tried to calm herself. After all, he was right. This was ridiculous. And where did she think she was going? It was just the two of them on this entire island for all she knew. There was only one way out of here, and that was on the *Mary Bernice*. She took a deep breath, willing her frantic pulse to slow. Then she raised her head

and met his eyes. He was angry still, but Kimberly could
see genuine bewilderment, too.

"Well?" he demanded.

She threw him a defiant glance. She knew her cheeks,
as they grew hot, betrayed her.

He looked at her for a moment longer, puzzled, and
then his eyes narrowed suddenly as though a thought
had just struck him, and his hard hands tightened on
her shoulders. "Oh, Lord! You're not . . . you're not a
virgin, are you?"

"It's no crime!" she yelled. Then, toweringly angry
that he'd had the insufferable gall to ask her such a
question, as if the answer had anything to do with what
had happened, as if the answer could possibly excuse his
actions or account for hers, she took a step back and
shoved his chest as hard as she could. Mike swore as he
was knocked off balance. She took the chance while she
had it and ran again.

This time Mike took her down with a flying tackle,
and they rolled over and over in the soft moss, she
fighting with every ounce of strength she had to escape
him, he trying to protect himself from her flailing fists
and knees and trap her securely under his body at the
same time.

Finally spent, Kimberly lay still, Mike's weight
pressing her down into the moss, his eyes gleaming in
male triumph.

"You can't get away from me that easily," he panted.
"And you can't get away from whatever it is you're
running from, either. I won't let you."

They were both out of breath. Kimberly turned her
face away, and tears seeped from under her closed lids.
For a long time they lay like that, Kimberly protected
from Mike's full weight by the springiness of the moss

they were on. Gradually their breathing slowed, but Kimberly's tears continued to flow, hot on her cool cheeks. She shuddered, a deep release from tension, then became aware of Mike's hand, gentle at her brow, smoothing back the tendrils of hair that stuck to her damp skin. She turned back to him and opened her eyes.

"Ah . . . Kimberly . . ." She met his eyes, tawny and dark and full of a tenderness she'd only dreamed of, and something else, the glow of purpose, desire—and pain, too.

"Don't cry, my beautiful woman with shining hair," he whispered, his voice thick with feeling. He bent and kissed her cheek gently where the tears had run. "Please don't cry. I would never hurt you. Don't you know that? Never!"

His lips moved from her cheek to her closed eyelids, soft, warm and firm. He brushed his mouth gently across hers, barely touching her, and her lips parted instinctively. But he didn't kiss her.

He raised himself higher on his elbows to take more of his weight and looked down at her, her smooth, pale body against his, legs to legs, hips to hips, belly to belly. Only a scrap of black fabric and his swimming trunks separated them in this magical forest, on this soft bed of moss. Here he was, with the woman of his dreams in his arms. It was a fantasy come true. They were perfect together; he'd always known they would be.

He ran his hand down her body, smoothing her skin lightly, caressing, soothing, gentling her after her storm of emotion. "I want to look at you," he whispered, and she grew still under his hands, exquisitely aware of his body against hers. He lifted her shoulders slightly and reached behind to unfasten her bikini top. Then he slid

it from her shoulders, smooth as silk, and put it to one
side, gazing down at her breasts. It was an action as
natural, as unconscious as breathing, here in this pri-
meval forest.

"You're so beautiful, Kimberly," he whispered. He
touched the curve of one breast lightly, and she trembled. "So beautiful, so perfect..." Then he bent his
head to kiss her cheek. "I want you, Kimberly. And I
know you want me, too," he said, his voice low, his
tongue tracing the delicate curve of her ear, sending a
shudder of delight through her body.

No, she shook her head from side to side, afraid to
trust her voice.

He frowned slightly, looking deep into her eyes. His
eyes were warm and golden and she trusted him instinctively. She knew he would never hurt her.

"You want me, Kimberly. You know you do." He
bent to her throat and kissed the smooth skin there.
"Do I have to show you? Again?"

She tried to cover her breasts, push him away from
her, but he swept her hands away and pressed her to the
ground, his bare chest rough against her smoothness,
her softness, and Kimberly felt the world spin as his
mouth took hers. Hands that she'd raised to push him
away reached up to pull him down to her, to hold him
as tightly as though he were life itself. Oh, Lord, what
was happening to her? She wanted this man with a deep
and terrible need she had never dreamed she possessed.

Mike's kiss deepened, seeking, searching, until he
found what he was looking for—her instinctive need for
him, only him among all men. And he knew it; he'd always known it.

When she was moaning, deep in her throat, her hands
and mouth caressing him until he shuddered, his con-

trol wavering, he took a ragged breath and raised his head, looking down at her, his nostrils flaring slightly.

"You want me, Kimberly," he said, his voice low and triumphant. It wasn't a question. She nodded, her eyes filled with some emotion he recognized as desire, and something else that sent a needle-sharp prick of fear through him. "Then tell me, damn it! Say it, Kimberly."

"I do want you, Mike. But..." Her voice was barely above a whisper, and then she bit her lip, holding back her words.

The satisfaction he wanted to feel, needed to feel, as he finally forced the truth from her wasn't there. He'd needed to force her. This woman, the woman he'd only dreamed of ever holding in his arms, felt the same things he was feeling but, for some reason, she was denying it with every stubborn fiber of her body. It should have been perfect; but it wasn't perfect at all. Mike frowned.

He kissed her again tenderly once, then with all the fierce passion of his unbridled spirit, and she clung to him. But it made no difference. Something within her held back.

"It's no good, is it?" he asked with a wry smile.

She shook her head, her eyes filling with quick tears again, and he shifted, rolling over so that he held her in his arms, cradled against the side of his chest, her head on his shoulder. Above them the lush green canopy of the coastal rain forest swayed gently in the breeze off Hecate Strait.

"Tell me about it, Kimberly," he said, his voice gentle.

She sniffed loudly and felt the low rumble of laughter through the solid wall of his chest. His arm tightened around her. "I'm...I'm afraid, Mike," she began, her voice little more than a whisper.

"Afraid! Of me?"

"A little. And, well...other things." She couldn't tell him that she'd sworn to herself that she'd never fall in love with a fisherman. Who was talking about love? All Mike wanted was an affair, a brief, explosive sharing of each other's bodies and then—*ciao*. That was the modern thing to do, wasn't it? But it wasn't Kimberly's way.

"I—I guess I'm a little old-fashioned."

"In other words you're holding out for marriage before you hop into bed with a man." His tone was flat and deliberately crude.

She hesitated, then nodded. Yes, she supposed that was what it amounted to, when you got right down to it. She hadn't particularly valued her virginal status; in fact, it had been more or less incidental as she'd put all her energies into the research career she'd chosen, the first of her family who'd ever done anything but fish or end up married to a fisherman. She hadn't given the matter too much thought before, but maybe that was why she'd never allowed anyone to get too close to her, had never even been tempted to make love with a man outside of marriage—until now.

If Mike thought she was being ridiculously old-fashioned, then all the better. Perhaps now he'd respect her wish to be left alone. She couldn't take much more of this: her resolve had already been thoroughly shaken by his kisses and caresses.

Mike was silent for a long time, then he sighed deeply, and she felt him withdraw. The intense intimacy of a few moments ago evaporated abruptly, and she felt unaccountably bereft.

"Well, I sure as hell don't want marriage," he said. His tone was very hard. "That's not what I had in mind at all."

Kimberly felt a sudden chill and sat up, reaching to retrieve her bikini top. She tied it with trembling fingers, aware that Mike was watching her every move.

"I was thinking more along the lines of two consenting adults who might enjoy a week or so together, offering each other pleasure—pleasure of the body and of the spirit." He raised one eyebrow mockingly. "Playing grown up." He sat up, then got to his feet and pulled her up with him.

"I'm not proposing!" she said, suddenly indignant, realizing at the same time how childish her assumed holdout for marriage must have sounded.

"No. Of course you're not."

His voice held a hint of laughter, which angered her. "And I don't have to justify myself to you, Mike Steele. I don't owe you any explanations and—" She knew she was right, but Mike's mocking expression disconcerted her and she struggled for words.

"No, of course you don't," he repeated, but she could hear the sarcasm. "I'm not trying to talk you into an affair with me, Kimberly. Lord knows, I haven't come to that yet. I just thought you might have changed your mind in the past week or so about sticking quite so hard to the rule book." He raised one eyebrow and smiled, his eyes searching hers. "My mistake."

He took a deep breath. "Look, Kimberly, you do crazy things to me, and I guess I let my feelings get a little out of hand. I apologize for putting pressure on you if that's what you thought I was doing. It won't happen again." Then he tipped up her chin with one finger. "No hard feelings?"

She shook her head. Mike smiled and reached up to pluck a few lumps of moss out of her disheveled hair, and she felt her heartbeat quicken, as always.

But the quick squeeze of her shoulders that he gave her before he went for the dinghy said it all: they were friends again, nothing more. He'd accepted her explanation—feeble though it was—and anything else between them was absolutely, definitely out.

Prince Rupert was a bustling little town a few hundred miles from the Alaska Panhandle that couldn't seem to make its mind up whether or not to jump into the harbor altogether and be done with it. Even its airport was oriented more to the sea than the land, situated as it was on an island, and the harbor was full of the everyday bustle of northern coastal commerce: oceangoing ships loading grain and coal, the gleaming white yachts and cruisers of the wealthy, the clang and ring of steel on steel from the boatyards, the bristling masts and colorful gear of the fishboats tied up at the cannery, and the buzz and scurry of seaplanes, taxiing here and there and looking more like lost and bewildered waterbugs than the vital lifeline of the north that they were.

Mike had tied up the *Mary Bernice* to the wharf at Waldo's Boatyard after off-loading his salmon and Kimberly had changed into a skirt and T-shirt and hurried up the hill. She was meeting Harry "Coho" Jenkins for lunch.

"Got your sea legs back, girl?" came the hearty roar over the lunchtime clatter of cutlery and crockery as soon as Kimberly opened the screen door to Marie's Good Eats.

"Uncle Harry!" With a squeal of delight Kimberly threw her arms around the burly fisherman and was nearly crushed in his huge embrace. She blinked back quick tears of pleasure, then raised her face to plant a couple of quick, loud kisses on the rough, unshaven cheek.

"How's that boy treatin' ya, Kimmie?" he growled. He pulled out a chair for her and shouted to the waitress to bring them a couple of coffees, then sat down across from her and leaned forward, taking her slim hands in his large paws. "Ya look good, Kimmie, ya know that? Real good. Trolling must agree with ya. Where's Mike?"

"Down at Waldo's. He said he might be up later to join us." She gave him an impish grin, her pleasure at seeing him shining from her eyes, then looked down and stirred her coffee. "You're a sly one, Uncle Harry, you are. Wonder where I got the idea the famous Big Mike Steele was an old geezer like you?" She laughed out loud as he looked just about as sheepish as she'd ever seen Coho Jenkins look. "I nearly went back to Vancouver when I found out what you'd pulled off."

He roared with laughter. "You didn't know any more about it than he did, girl. Ya think he'd have taken you on if I'd told him you were a woman? No bloody way!" Harry waved away the waitress, ordering steaks for both of them before Kimberly had even had a chance to examine the dog-eared menu.

"I gathered that. So what's he got against woman?" Kimberly's question was light, but every sense was suddenly, keenly, attuned to Harry's answer.

"Just about as much as you've got against fishermen" was his prompt answer. "Both of you are just plumb mule-headed in my books. A couple of weeks together'll do you both good, straighten you out right smart.'' He winked and grinned. ''I'd lay a bottle of rum on it if I had a taker.''

Kimberly grinned as she cut into her steak. Uncle Harry had been like this as long as she could remember, and she was glad that some things in life, at least, never changed. He was a take-charge fisherman who'd never married, although Kimberly had heard rumors as a child that he'd held a torch all his life for some woman who wouldn't have him. Kimberly didn't know if it was true—there certainly wasn't the least bit of melancholy about Coho Jenkins—but the story had always given him an aura of faint romance in her eyes. A lost love, and his attachment to the sea. Then she frowned. Uncle Harry was a trollerman, too.

''So. You know my story, Uncle Harry. What's Mike's?'' She took a bite of salad and chewed thoughtfully as the older fisherman filled her in.

''Once bitten, twice shy,'' Coho said, leaning forward. ''Don't suppose he told ya, eh?'' Kimberly shook her head. ''Well, no, he wouldn't. Fact is, he got himself almost married once, daughter of one of his mother's friends—mama was all for it, I heard—and the young lady in question threw him over when he refused to quit fishin'.''

Kimberly's eyes were round with surprise. ''Quit fishing?'' Who was she? What did she look like? Why did Coho's information drop like large, cold stones into her lighthearted, happy mood? Why should she care about an old romance of Mike Steele's?

''Mike's family had always figured he'd take over the helm of the family business when his dad died but, hell, he's no pen pusher. He tried it for a while after college, for his mother's sake, but his heart wasn't in it.''

Family business? College? She raised her eyebrow in inquiry.

"Steele Seafoods. You must have heard of them. Big plant in Victoria."

Kimberly nodded, then swallowed slowly. Steele Seafoods was the biggest cannery and exporter of Canadian fish products in the province. She'd never for a moment associated the last name of her boss with a background like that. No wonder he didn't mind taking a day or two off when the salmon were running—he obviously didn't need the money to meet a backbreaking boat mortgage like most fishermen. Kimberly's blue eyes clouded and she frowned.

"I don't get it, Uncle Harry. If he's got an outfit like that behind him, what's he doing out fishing?" She jumped in her seat when the big man opposite her slammed his beefy fist on the table, making the glasses rattle and the cutlery jump.

"Damn it, Kimberly!" he roared. "You oughta know better than to ask me a fool question like that. He's got brine in his blood, damn it, just like every other troller-man. A man like that can't just throw in the towel and hunker down to some desk job in the city. It just ain't in him." Coho's old blue eyes bored into hers. "I woulda thought you of all people would know that."

She nodded, then blinked and looked down at her plate. Uncle Harry was right. Everything he said was true. The call of the sea came first with some men. It had been like that for her father and her brothers, and that was exactly why she was never getting tangled up with a fisherman. She was glad Uncle Harry had unwittingly clarified her position for her; these past few days spent with Mike Steele had muddled her resolve.

Still, she felt a faint sadness and sense of regret for what might have been—maybe. Mike had made a conscious choice and was prepared to live with the consequences, but what about the loneliness? He couldn't control that. He was a strong, passionate man who loved life more than anyone she'd ever met, and yet he'd chosen to live alone. It stirred her deeply.

"More coffee?" The plump waitress held out the pot, and Kimberly nodded absently. "How about a piece of apple pie? Nice and hot with plenty of ice cream?" Kimberly started to shake her head, but Coho broke in.

"Ah, sure she'll have a piece. Don't get no cookin' like our Marie's on the *Mary B,* I'll wager." He winked at the waitress and reached out to put his arm around her waist. With the ease of long practice she nimbly avoided the gesture and flapped the menu playfully at Coho's grizzled head before heading back to the kitchen.

"You never finished telling me about Mike's big romance. What happened?" Kimberly was more than curious. She just hoped she'd get all the details from Uncle Harry before Mike arrived. She knew she'd never get a word out of him.

"Rosa was her name. Prettiest thing I ever saw—dark curly hair, beautiful brown eyes." With sudden pain Kimberly remembered Mike's warning when she'd gone aboard the troller, the bald statement that she wasn't his type, anyway.

"But, unfortunately, she had sawdust for brains, if you ask me. She told Mike it was her or the sea. He stuck with the sea, and she went after his cousin, Alexander. Sandy runs the company now, although Mike's still the major shareholder. A piece of woman's work all right—cousins on the outs and they damn near grew up together like brothers. Mike's mother is put out with him, and Mike's down on women in general.

"Only winner I can see out of the whole nasty business is little Rosa Steele. She's happy as a clam, two fine kiddies, as much money as she can spend, a great big house on the bay and a good-looking husband padlocked to a desk in Victoria. Damn near heaven, I'd say!" Coho snorted in disgust and Kimberly laughed.

When Mike shouldered open the screen door ten minutes later, Kimberly was laughing and gossiping with Coho, fitting easily into the boisterous camaraderie of the fishermen's diner and yet standing out like a ray of palest, fragile sunshine in the crowd. He drew in his breath with a pain that startled him with its intensity.

Damn! he thought, and deliberately set his features in a mask of indifference. There was no doubt about it—the sooner this particular deckhand left the *Mary Bernice,* the better off her skipper would be. And, in the end, that was what mattered. All he could do was mess up her life—and his.

He'd thought it over carefully while he'd made the few repairs necessary to the *Mary B*'s gear. Word had already spread among the close-knit fishing community that Mike Steele had taken on a long-legged blonde as deckhand, and even his terse responses to the occasional teasing inquiry hadn't stopped the guffaws and winks.

That was the trouble with fishermen: ultimately they were cut from the same cloth, and you had to be part of the same network if you wanted to survive with them. It was a man's world. Mike knew his reputation was the only thing that kept them from ribbing him unmercifully. They knew he walked alone—always had—and kept his own counsel, and they respected that. He was of them, but he wasn't one of them. Yet they knew he could be counted on to lend a hand, whether it was helping to organize a local co-op to sell fish or mending gear for a fellow fisherman who'd been laid up sick a few days before the season started or taking up a collection for a new widow.

Still...Mike had thought as he'd helped Waldo McPherson pry back the left hold door that had been sticking, if they knew his reading material aboard the troller ran more to Keats and Shelley than to girlie magazines, they'd have his hide pegged to the cannery wall.

It had taken longer than he'd expected arranging for the welding job at Waldo's and, once, just after he'd made up his mind that Kimberly definitely would have to go back to Vancouver, he'd felt a flash of panic as the thought had struck him that maybe she'd already packed her duffel bag and left. His heart in his mouth, he'd leaped aboard the troller and swung down into the cabin to stand, heart hammering, in the aisle, looking at her things still strewn about her bunk. And then he'd known for certain that she would have to leave; there was no other way.

"Mike!" He nodded at several acquaintances as he made his way between the tables in the crowded diner.

"How's fishin'? Catchin' anything in the way of—" here the bearded young fisherman looked at his colleagues around the table, grinning "—fish, Mike?"

There was a roar of laughter at the table, and a great deal of interest followed Mike Steele to the table in the corner by the window. He'd nodded and grinned good-naturedly. What else could he do?

"Well, well, how are ya, Mike?" The two men nodded at each other in the extremely brief and offhand way that men reserve for their most-loved male friends, and Coho Jenkins waved Mike into the chair beside Kimberly. She shifted slightly as though to move as far away from him as possible, an action Mike didn't miss. A muscle moved slightly in his jaw.

She was dressed in a yellow skirt and striped T-shirt, wrinkled from a couple of weeks stuffed into a boat locker, but he thought he'd never seen a woman look more beautiful. Not that he looked at her. Not directly.

"Coho, you old son of a gun. What you up to in Rupert?"

The two friends began a brisk discussion of the vagaries of government regulations, brass lures and the price of chinook salmon, ignoring Kimberly, and she looked around the room casually, excruciatingly aware of Mike's jean-clad thigh so near hers at the small table. Absently she played with her coffee spoon. Well, it was all over now. She'd pack her bags after lunch. Mike had never changed his mind about getting rid of her as a deckhand—not really—and now that they were in Prince Rupert she could easily catch a flight home and he could easily pick up another deckhand for the rest of the season.

After the day they'd spent at Lyall Island, who could blame him? He must have realized he'd been saddled with not only a woman who was plagued by ghosts from the past that she was still unwilling or unable to talk about, but a woman who was so unsure of her own femininity and sexuality that she couldn't—or wouldn't—recognize the strong attraction that existed between them and deal with it in a mature and healthy way. She was twenty-four, for Pete's sake, she was more or less an accidental virgin, and she was still scared to death of the feelings aroused in her by the most attractive man she'd ever met. A man who would conveniently disappear from her life at the end of the salmon season.

She shot a quick sideways glance at his handsome profile. Had ever a better opportunity existed to explore her own feelings as a woman? What had he said—to offer each other pleasures of the body and spirit. She thought fleetingly of the beautiful Rosa. Had they been lovers?

No, she thought with a frown, Kimberly Bowring was still far too uptight and rigidly upright to play by the kind of rules Mike Steele used. The point was—he made up his own rules, and she never had.

"So where ya headin' now, Mike? Come on, ya can tell a friend!" Coho said, slapping the table as he grinned at Mike's skeptical look. Fishermen were notorious for trying to find out surreptitiously from each other where the fish were biting. Thus the elaborate codes on the marine radio between partners and friends. No one wanted the entire North Pacific fishing fleet to follow him to his favorite spot.

"Thought I might head south. I know a good place just north of Rivers Inlet." Mike cradled the coffee mug in his large hands, hands that were scarred, tanned and lean. Strong hands, but sensitive, the hands of an artist and a warrior. She thought of that night she'd spent on the troller's deck, watching Mike's small camp fire onshore where he'd spent the night alone under the stars on Lyall Island, the way the Haida might have done a hundred years before, then wrenched her eyes away to answer Coho's repeated question.

"No, er, no, I've never been to Rivers Inlet, Uncle Harry. And—" she glanced nervously at Mike, who seemed to be ignoring her "—I don't think I'll be going, either. Mike's paying me off here and—"

"What?" Coho was astonished. This, apparently, wasn't part of his plan. "Paying you off? The season ain't over." He glared at his friend. "What's goin' on, Mike? Ain't she a damn fine deckhand?"

"The best."

"Can't she cook?"

"She can."

"Then what's the trouble?" Coho was getting redder by the minute. "Don't give me that tired old tune about women deckhands, young fella. This here salmon snatcher wasn't born yesterday, ya know!"

Mike regarded his old friend through narrowed eyes for a long moment. He couldn't have asked for a more perfect opportunity to bring up the subject. He lifted his mug to finish the dregs of coffee, glanced casually down into it and, to his complete astonishment, heard himself say, "Never said anything about paying off Bowring."

It was Kimberly's turn to regard Mike with dismay.

Coho chuckled, his face splitting into a toothy grin. "Well, there ya go. Ya got a job to finish off, Kimmie. Ya gonna take it?"

She felt a faint flush rising and looked up at Mike. He finally gave her a quick half-frowning, sideways glance that told her nothing, then held his empty mug up to catch the waitress's attention. He truly didn't seem to care one way or another. Well, what *was* she going to do? She hadn't thought it would come to this.

"Damn it, make up your mind, girl. Ya gonna take a chance with this fella for another coupla weeks, or am I gonna take you to the airport right now?"

"I—" She looked up at Mike, hoping for a clue about his real feelings, but his face was a mask of indifference. Maybe he really didn't care one way or the other. Maybe what she'd said on Lyall Island really had changed the way he regarded her. In that case... She bit her bottom lip nervously.

Casually Mike looked out the window at the bustle of harborfront activity, then leaned back in his chair and pulled a lure catalog out of his shirt pocket. He began to study it intently.

"I—I guess I'll stay, Uncle Harry," she finally said weakly.

And laughing, then, at the wild whoop Coho Jenkins let out, she didn't notice how Mike had sharply exhaled, then banged down his chair and stuffed the hitherto riveting display of lures unceremoniously back into his pocket.

Chapter Seven

The rest of the day passed very quickly. There were clothes to be washed and dried in the marina Laundromat, there were groceries to be purchased and stowed in the food larder and refrigerator, there was a last-minute telephone call to her mother in Steveston to tell her everything was going fine and not to worry.

That, Kimberly thought wryly as she hung up the receiver in the phone booth, just might be the most ambiguous statement of the year. But, amazingly, since she'd made the snap decision to stick out the rest of the season with Mike, she'd felt a burden had been lifted from her shoulders. Fate or whatever it was she'd been fighting for so long suddenly seemed to have switched sides. She felt more relaxed than she had for months. From now on, she decided, she'd concentrate on why she was aboard the *Mary Bernice* in the first place. The rest of the worries she'd leave to Mike.

Not that he looked as if he ever worried. In fact, that was one of the elusive qualities that set Mike Steele apart: he took life as it came, good and bad, and met each challenge as it presented itself. Worry was not part of his life.

"'Bye, darlin'." By late afternoon they were ready to leave Prince Rupert, and Kimberly hugged Coho Jenkins tightly, secretly happy that he'd cared enough about her to arrange this trip with Mike. As far as the therapy went—if that's what it was—it seemed to be working. She was far less apprehensive about being out on the water than she had been, and so far she'd only had one real panic attack. Even the nightmares seemed to be less frequent. Was she really beating her fears? Or was it just that she had such a faith in the *Mary B*'s skipper?

"Remember me to your mama when you get home." Coho grinned and gave her a last squeeze. "And don't let that sea cowboy give you too tough a time."

"I won't, Uncle Harry."

"And you, young fella," he said, slapping Mike on the shoulder, "you take care of my Kimmie. I don't want to hear anything I shouldn't, or you'll have me to answer to."

Mike shook his hand and grinned. "Don't worry, old man, she's in good hands."

"That's just what I'm afraid of!"

With more shouted farewells, Mike eased the troller away from her berth and carefully began picking his way through the harbor traffic. Finally they were clear, and Mike set a steady course south-southwest.

The evening meal was a subdued affair. Mike was preoccupied and silent and Kimberly was loath to draw him into conversation. Was he already regretting allowing her to finish out the season? She feigned a great deal of interest in the food on her plate—fried chicken and a Caesar salad she'd made from the fresh greens she'd purchased at a Prince Rupert supermarket—but, in fact, she had never felt less like eating.

Once she glanced up to find Mike regarding her intently. He looked away as soon as she met his gaze, pushed back his plate and swung up to the wheelhouse. A few moments later the *Mary Bernice* was steaming full speed ahead.

"Where are we going?" Kimberly finally ventured when she'd finished up the dishes and climbed up to the wheelhouse.

He hesitated, then gave her a narrow, sideways look. "Place I know."

"What's it called?"

"I don't think it's named on the charts," he said. "The Indians called it Water-Where-Big-Fish-Play." He gave her an enigmatic glance, and she knew she probably wouldn't be told any more about it.

"Are we fishing in the morning?" At least she'd like to know if she had to get her gear ready.

"Not the morning. Maybe the afternoon." Mike's attention was taken by a large bed of kelp that had materialized. He steered carefully around it, then resumed full speed. Wherever it was they were going, Michael Delano Steele was in his usual hurry.

Kimberly climbed back down and made up her bunk. She smiled once as she lay there, a little surprised to realize how warm and secure she felt in the gently rocking vessel, with the monotonous rumble of the big diesels lulling her to sleep and with a man she trusted completely at the helm. That's because he's a living legend, she thought, yawning. She felt safe because she knew he knew what he was doing up there. But that didn't account for the overwhelming sense of finally coming home that overtook her just as she fell asleep.

When Kimberly awoke the next morning, the sun was streaming through the porthole nearest her bunk. It was quiet, absolutely quiet, and for a moment she lay there, thinking back to the dream, if she'd had one, that had awoken her. But what had awoken her hadn't been in her dream. There it was again—a faint mewing sound, then a soft splash, then a high-pitched squeak and a whistle. She lay there absolutely still. If she didn't know better, she'd say it was... Yes, there was no doubt about it.

She glanced over to Mike's bunk. It was empty. Without a thought to getting dressed, she scrambled up the ladder in her nightie.

"Oh!" she gasped. She couldn't believe her eyes. Killer whales! Dozens of them around the boat.

"Shh!" Mike was stretched out flat on his belly on the afterdeck, chin on hands, silently watching. He gestured to her to join him.

She crept quietly forward and wriggled up to lie flat beside him on the deck. Her hair was all sleep-tangled, her face needed a wash, but she didn't care. Killer whales! Wild orcas, glistening black-and-white bodies knifing through the clear water of the little bay and breaching all around the boat, blowing their spume in little puffs of vapor, the loud *smack-smack* of their blowholes opening and closing...

"Oh, Mike," she whispered, her voice trembling, her eyes filled with the prickle of tears, "I've never seen anything so wonderful, so... so beautiful."

"Shh," he said again, one finger to his lips, and then she noticed that he was bare-chested and not wearing much more than she was, only a pair of faded denim cutoffs.

He was right; the display of wild orcas in their glorious natural habitat was a sight too precious and rare to waste. Family groups cavorted together, and some of the pod rubbed up against the rocks at the side of the bay, unusual sandstone formations that reminded her of the rocks at Robson Bight, a well-known area where the black-and-white mammals had gathered for millennia. The area surrounding Robson Bight, where she'd planned to do her research, would someday—she hoped—be protected from the logger's saw as the government recognized the uniqueness of the Bight, and that it was worthy of protection and preservation.

For more than an hour she lay beside Mike, chin on hands, feeling the soft morning sun on her skin, her body nestled next to his on the sun-warmed deck, listening to the muffled squeals and chirps of the whales at play and the piercing cries of seabirds wheeling overhead. Uncle Harry was right—how could this man have lived indoors chained to a desk? Water-Where-Big-Fish-Play, she thought. How aptly named.

But this place wasn't on any map. No one knew much more of the literature on killer whales along this coast than Kimberly Bowring, and she'd never heard of this bay.

She realized then that this place was known only to a few—to Mike Steele and to the Indians who had most probably told him about it. And he'd brought her here to this special private place because he knew she'd respect it, and because he knew that she loved the great killer whales. Kimberly's eyes filled with quick tears of gratitude, and later—much later—she thought that perhaps it was then that she realized she'd fallen in love

with a trollerman, after all. Or perhaps she already
loved him, because later—much later—it seemed that
she had always loved him, that there had never been a
time before loving him.

"What's the matter?" Mike had seen the tears run
down her cheeks onto her tightly closed hands and then
onto the deck. He looked faintly perplexed.

"Oh, Mike," she breathed, turning to him, her face
radiant, "it's so wonderful, so special. Thank you for
giving me this. I—I'll never forget it."

Mike seemed embarrassed, and looked back out over
the shining water, frowning slightly. When he looked
back at her, his expression was faintly hooded. "I'm
glad I could give it to you, Kimberly" was all he said.

Then she put her head down gently on her arms and
wept—wept for the joy and pain she knew there would
be in loving this man; for the pain of having grown up
all at once, just now, for that was what had happened;
for the wasted lives of the father and brother she would
never see again; for the generations of women in her
family who'd loved their men and lost them to the sea.

Mike made no move to touch her, although the pain
he felt at feeling her strangled sobs and shaking shoulders beside him was etched on his face. Her grief had
been a long time coming. Too long. Maybe now . . .

"Are you ready to talk about it, Kimberly?" he said
finally, softly, turning to her on the deck, raising his
upper body on one elbow and looking down at her.
smiled slightly as she wiped her reddened eyes on her
sleeve, then stared in alarm at herself as she realized she
was still wearing her nightgown. He dug into his pocket
and handed her a handkerchief. She blew her nose vigorously and he smiled again.

As though aware of something dramatic taking place on the black-hulled intruder, several killer whales stood in a phalanx on their tails a dozen yards away, heads inclined toward the *Mary B* as though to watch the show.

"Yes, I—I think I am, Mike," Kimberly said, biting her lip. She realized how close she was—finally—to confiding in someone who would understand, someone who risked his life on the sea every season of the year. But could she really unburden herself to Mike? He was far from the kindly old man of the sea she'd once envisaged.

Mike guessed at the reason for her hesitation and sat up. Even now she needed time. "I'll go make some coffee, eh? Then you can get dressed and tell me about it." He gave her a quick, friendly smile, hoping his eyes wouldn't betray him.

It was driving him crazy to have her so close to him and so far from him at the same time. Every nerve was painfully, excruciatingly aware of her slim, soft body beside him, the scent of her warm, sun-kissed skin, the silky texture of her sleep-mussed hair...

He was perilously close to just taking her into his arms and covering her tear-smeared face with kisses until she smiled again, until she reached for him, until she... He wanted to toss her nightgown into the sea and take her right here on the sun-warmed deck with the killer whales breaching all around them. Could there ever be a more beautiful place to teach her the ways of love between a man and a woman?

He sighed deeply and got to his feet, reaching down to pull her up lightly. It wasn't possible. Not now, not ever. He turned and made his way down to the galley, running both hands through his hair in frustration. How the hell had his life gotten so complicated all of a sudden?

Gradually, over the course of the next couple of days, Kimberly told Mike everything. She relived the painful memories of the accident, of how she'd clung to the log in the icy water, afraid that every wave would be the one that swamped her, that would separate her from the only thing that gave her a slim chance of survival. And how she'd screamed the names of her father and brother over and over until her throat was raw. How she'd been tempted to swim for them, to see if she could find them, injured perhaps, and help them to share her log. But her terror at losing sight of the log, the only hope in a savage, storm-tossed world—her fear and the thread of common sense that told her that it was far, far too late for her father and brother—prevented her from trying. For two years she'd lived with the terrible guilt that perhaps she could have, should have, done something more.

She knew that Mike understood, in a way that Dr. Gilling or her mother never could. When he held her in his arms during her storms of emotions over the next couple of days, it was as though he had become the one ray of hope and strength and support in a black, painful world.

Then, when the tears had finally run dry, Mike told her of the times he had been afraid, too—the time he was adrift in a lifeboat in the North Pacific for three days, the times he'd been caught in treacherous riptides in rocky channels and had barely saved himself and the *Mary B.* All men who lived at sea lived with fear in their hearts and the joy that came of conquering that fear, he told her as gently as he could, watching as she went from hopelessness and guilt to believing him and believing in him.

He noted the signs of her growing faith in him, and it troubled him deeply. Still, what had he expected? He was taking the role of confidant and confessor, and he could hardly be surprised if she repaid him with gratitude. But gratitude was not what he wanted from Kimberly.

Then, one night, he was put to the test. Kimberly had cried out during one of her nightmares, which had returned with a vengeance. He'd gone to her bunk to reassure her, and in her confused and frightened state she'd clung to him, both arms around his neck.

"Hold me, Mike," she whispered. "Don't leave me!"

"Kimberly..."

"Don't let me go. Please."

Her grip tightened and he lifted her into his arms. She put her head against his shoulder and sighed deeply. Had she gone back to sleep? "Kimberly!"

"Mmm..."

She'd nodded off again. Damn! Maybe if he just held her for a few moments he could put her back gently and she'd stay asleep. But it didn't work. As soon as he bent to put her down, she moaned and clung to him even tighter. With a sigh of exasperation and frustration, he lifted her onto his bed and rolled in beside her.

This was agony. The woman he'd wanted in his bed almost from the day he'd met her was exactly where he wanted her, and there was nothing he could do about it. Her pale, silky hair in disarray against his neck and mouth, her soft breasts pressing against the side of his chest as he held her in his arms, the sweet, clean scent of her in his nostrils—it was more than he could bear. No man, no matter how pure and disinterested he told himself his motives were, should have to put up with temptation like this. Nightmare or no nightmare, she had to get back into her own bed, or soon he wouldn't be responsible for the consequences.

"Kimberly, sweetheart, wake up." Her only response was to curl tighter against him and press her lips into the side of his neck. He groaned. She was breathing deeply and evenly, sound asleep. "Kimberly!" he whispered loudly in her ear, shaking her a little.

She raised her head, and her eyes widened slowly. "Oh! Who . . . how did I get in here?"

He would have laughed if it hadn't been so damnably painful. "You've got to get back into your own bed. I can't take much more of this."

"Of what?" Her voice was thick with sleep and her question seemed totally innocent.

"Having you in my arms, for God's sake," he growled, shifting so that he loomed over her. She stared up at him with wide eyes. "In my bed. Exactly where I've wanted you ever since you came aboard this damn boat! I'm a man of enormous self-control, Kimberly, but I've just about reached my limit. You've got to get out of here." This last was through gritted teeth.

Kimberly sat up and swung her feet over the side. Her bed felt cold and unfriendly after the warmth and comfort of Mike's. But she went to sleep again with a small smile on her face: the man she loved didn't love her, but he wanted her. Badly. Perhaps that was enough, after all.

The next morning Mike got a radio call from a government fisheries official informing him that the salmon quota had been filled for that season, and as of noon

Pacific Standard Time, all trolling gear had to be clear of the water and rendered inoperable. He spent the afternoon working on his gear, and when he did speak to Kimberly, he was short with her, snapping out gruff answers to her questions and generally behaving like a bear with a sore paw.

What's bugging him? Kimberly thought as she made coffee for their afternoon break. It couldn't be because the salmon season had been cut short. She knew now that Mike didn't depend upon fishing for his livelihood; it was just something he had to do. And now he'd be able to take her into a port where she could get off the boat after all. That should make him happy, Kimberly thought with small twinge of pain as she poured the boiling water into the mugs to warm them. She wondered if that was what he'd wanted to do all along, as he'd once said. Maybe he'd just kept her on at Prince Rupert because he felt sorry for her. Uncle Harry, no doubt, had given him some idea of why she'd hired on with him in the first place.

Face it. He's probably sexually frustrated, too, she decided with a faint twinge of guilt that she knew she ought not to have felt. He'd admitted that he wanted more than her friendship....

Friendship! she scoffed to herself. Quit beating around the bush, Bowring. He's been perfectly frank— he wants to sleep with you. It's probably driving him crazy having an attractive woman on board who's made it clear that, first of all, she's not interested in an affair with him—or anyone—and, secondly, she's turned out to be an inexperienced virgin whom he probably wouldn't touch with a ten-foot pole, anyway.

Kimberly climbed up to the wheelhouse with the mugs and handed one to Mike. He muttered a gruff thanks and kept his dark head bent over the chart. She might not have been there.

He'd set the troller on a southerly course, and they were moving at a leisurely half speed. The sun was far to the west and the sunset was glorious: red and orange with great splashes of purple and pink over the distant mountains of Vancouver Island. Clouds covered the sky over the Pacific Ocean, and Kimberly felt a slight chill in the air.

She looked over at Mike and felt her heart give a great, slow kick as she studied his dark, brooding profile, the deceptively easy way he leaned against the chart table. That lazy stance gave no hint of the coiled reserves beneath the surface, the iron strength that could be galvanized into action the instant it was needed. He frowned as he studied the chart and made a few scratched calculations on a piece of paper.

He looked up suddenly, catching her study of him, and she quickly colored, turning to her coffee mug in confusion.

"Kimberly?"

"Yes?" She hoped he hadn't guessed at the feelings that must have been plain on her face.

"You ready to head home now?"

Startled, she looked up again. His tawny eyes met hers, deliberately cool, it seemed to her. "Why . . . yes, of course. Now that the season's over I guess I should get home as soon as I can." She tried to ignore the iciness that clutched her heart for a moment. "You can drop me off anywhere, Mike. Are you going into Hardy?"

Port Hardy was a small community on the northernmost tip of Vancouver Island. Mike could off-load his salmon there and she could catch a plane home.

"I could." He studied her for a moment, and she met his gaze, quietly, calmly. Then he went on, hesitating a little. "I, uh, I could take you back to Vancouver if you want. I'm heading to Victoria, anyway."

"Well, if that's—" Kimberly tried to quell the wild exhilaration that suddenly gripped her, chasing away the numbness. She'd be with him a few more days! He wasn't trying to get rid of her early!

"It's no trouble. It's only a little out of my way." That settled, Mike turned back to the chart and made another calculation. The tension in the small wheel-house had altered somehow. Then he glanced up and smiled, a wide grin that, to Kimberly's eyes at least, looked almost as ridiculously happy as she felt. "Mind if we stop off at Cortes on the way?"

Cortes Island was one of the northernmost Gulf Islands in the Strait of Georgia that separated Vancouver Island, with the capital city of Victoria at the southern end, from the mainland, where the city of Vancouver was located. She frowned a little. "What's on Cortes?"

"My house." He continued smiling.

"House!" Somehow she'd never thought of this man as having any other life than roaming the seas on his fishing boat. But, of course, he'd have a place to spend the winter, friends, perhaps even a steady girlfriend somewhere.... She really knew almost nothing about him.

"Yeah." He studied her for a long moment, wishing for the thousandth time that things weren't the way they were between them. He'd never dreamed he'd want anything more than what he already had: the *Mary Bernice* and the freedom that went with being his own man, needing no one and no one needing him. But now this small determined woman, with hair like finest spun silver, and bones as delicate as a bird, with eyes like the sea and the sky all run together and the softest lips he'd ever kissed, had come into his world and turned everything upside down. The sooner she got out of his life, the better. So why did he keep thinking of ways to keep her aboard? He didn't want—didn't dare—to examine his motives too closely.

"I don't mind," she said finally, airily, with a shrug. "I'll be getting home earlier than I'd thought, anyway. It's not as if anyone's expecting me."

She grinned, an impish grin that made him want to take the two strides between them and crush her into his arms and keep her there forever. But, instead, with nothing more than a grunt of acknowledgment, he turned his back on her and leaned over the charts again.

All at once Kimberly made up her mind about something that had been hovering at the edge of her consciousness for a long time—perhaps since she'd stepped aboard. It was crazy, it was dangerous, it was completely out of character, but she suddenly discovered she wanted it more than she'd ever wanted anything in her life.

Maybe it was the sense of euphoria she'd felt since she'd unburdened herself to Mike and realized that she was strong enough finally to come to grips with her fears about the sea. Maybe it was recognizing that she'd come of age, in a way, and needed to prove it to herself. A rite of passage. Maybe she didn't need to look any farther than her own heart for a reason: more than anything she yearned to banish the dark loneliness from the face of the man she loved, even if it was for just one night.

Whatever the reasons, it didn't much matter: Kimberly had made up her mind to seduce Mike Steele.

Chapter Eight

The moon streamed through the portholes and brushed the inside of the troller with silver. Kimberly lay in her bed in an agony of indecision. It was one thing to make up her mind to climb into Mike's bunk; it was quite another to do it.

She had showered and washed her hair and dried it and put on a clean nightie. The nightie she'd hesitated over—somehow serviceable cotton had never figured in this sort of fantasy before—but had finally put it on. This wasn't a fantasy. The man in the next bunk was real flesh and blood, real passion and real needs, and after tonight she wouldn't be able to think otherwise ever again.

Why was she doing this? Kimberly rubbed damp palms on the sheet. Sure she was nervous, but she wanted to do it, she had to do it, it was part of the letting go. And there was no question—ever—of a future with Mike, anyway. Just once she wanted the freedom to touch him all over, to hold him, to share deep kisses with him, to yield the secrets of her innocence to him.

The fact that she knew she'd never see him again after they got into port had something to do with it, too, she admitted a little uncomfortably. Was that unfair, perhaps manipulative? Certainly not to her—it was exactly the way she wanted it to be, she told herself. To him? But he'd always said there was no room for a woman in his life. He wanted her; he'd admitted that. But his need was a fierce hunger of the flesh only, she thought with a touch of sadness, and emotional and physical hunger that could be sated with a brief, intense affair with a woman from time to time. Mike had been blunt: marriage was not for him.

Kimberly tensed, listening. There was no sound from the bunk opposite, and it was getting late. She squinted at her travel alarm. Half an hour past midnight! Mike had stayed up on the deck a long time after she'd gone to bed and she'd almost fallen asleep waiting. The haunting strains of his harmonica had drifted down to her in the velvety darkness and had almost moved her to tears. Why was that sound so much a part of lonely men?

But finally he had made his way down, and she'd heard the muffled sounds of his preparations, followed by the darkness and silence that indicated sleep. He'd been asleep for an hour already while she'd tried to gather her courage.

Kimberly sat up and threw off her blanket. Quietly as she could, she pushed back the curtain that separated her bunk from the open cabin. Then she slipped out of bed and stood there for a moment, shivering a little as she felt the cool night air on her heated skin.

Mike was turned half away from her in sleep, one arm thrown up in a vulnerable gesture above his head. She saw the smooth rise and fall of his bare chest, gleaming in the soft moon's glow. His features were half shadowed by his upflung arm, but there was no doubt that he was sound asleep.

Sudden doubts clutched at her but, heart hammering, she reached up to undo the shoulder strap of her nightgown before she could change her mind. Anyone would think you were going to your own execution, she thought, stifling a sudden desire to giggle hysterically by biting down hard on her bottom lip. It hurt and, as she blinked back the tears of pain, Kimberly changed her mind about taking off her nightgown. When it came right down to it, she just couldn't remove that last barrier, inconsequential though it was.

Taking a deep breath, she stole closer to Mike's bunk, lifted up his duvet and quietly slipped in beside him. She lay there stiffly on her back and let out a slow, agonized breath. She was afraid to look at him. She was almost afraid to breathe. But he hadn't moved a muscle.

Again she felt the quick flutter of hysteria rise. What if she spent the whole night beside him and he never even knew she was there?

She lay still for a few moments, allowing her breathing to return to normal, gradually becoming aware of the soft sounds of the water slapping against the hull, the far-off cry of a night raptor, the creak of swaying gear. She became aware of the solid heat of Mike's body beside her, not quite touching her, but reaching out to her with its warmth. Carefully she eased nearer, drawn to his heat and the unfamiliar male scent of his skin and hair. She wanted to touch him; she didn't dare.

Kimberly felt a rising excitement within her. Cautiously, slowly, she reached out and touched her lips lightly to his bare shoulder, inhaling the scent of his skin. He moved a little but didn't awaken and, emboldened, Kimberly moved closer until she could feel the length of his hip and leg against hers, the solid barrier of his chest against hers. She moved her mouth against his skin, slowly savoring the forbidden pleasure, examining with almost a sense of detachment the tiny ripples of sensation that swirled through her own body. She could hear, and feel, the slow, deep thud of his heart beneath the muscle and bone, the slight catch of his breath as he slept.

Then, without any warning at all, Mike rolled over and gathered her into his arms. Kimberly's heart hammered in her ears. Mike's arms had gone around her, and he'd thrown one leg over both of hers so that she was trapped in a natural embrace, her head tucked under his chin. She realized, with a ridiculous sense of relief, that he was wearing some sort of lower garment. Not—she blushed furiously in the dark—that it made a whole lot of difference. She could feel every part of him pressed intimately against her.

For a long time they lay like that. Kimberly hoped that her pulse would slow, but it didn't. If anything, every nerve became more excruciatingly alive. Finally she moved slightly, unable anymore to remain still.

Mike moved, too. And, as easily and naturally as lovers clasp hands, his mouth covered hers in the darkness and they were joined. Kimberly shuddered at the sensation. His hands moved to stroke her body slowly, from shoulder to hip, to mold her even closer against him. His lips moved over hers with an even, gentle pressure that sought her secrets and gave his. Breathless, Kimberly moaned his name over and over against his mouth, and he drew her whispers deep into his body.

Like a woman who finally realizes there is nothing more stopping her from loving, she reached up to pull Mike even closer to her, to hold him even tighter in her arms. Then she felt his hands moving over her hips and stroking, smoothing around to her breasts, taking one soft mound in his hand, the jutting peak pressing against his hard palm, and she cried out at the sheer stabbing pleasure of his touch.

He kissed her again and again in silence until Kimberly was nearly wild with feeling. She moaned and writhed against him, desperate to feel his skin against hers, wishing she'd taken off her nightgown when she'd had the chance.

"Oh, angel," Mike whispered against her mouth, "is this a dream, or am I really holding you in my arms?"

"It's not a dream, Mike," she managed, gasping as he caressed the delicate shell of her ear with his tongue.

"My angel, my sweet angel," he murmured over and over, kissing her face, her throat, the soft swell of her breast above the ruffled neckline of her nightgown. "I've wanted this for so long, my beautiful Woman-With-The-Shining-Hair. I've wanted you forever," he said in a harsh whisper, shifting to slide one arm under her hips to draw her against him. Kimberly gasped and trembled as she felt his hard body against hers, his desire for her unmistakable.

Then his mouth moved to her breast, and she cried out again, arching against him as he drew her aroused nipple into his mouth through the thin fabric.

"Oh, Mike, Mike..." She couldn't say anything more as she tried to deal with the crashing sensations of pleasure that swept through her. Joy, joy that she was with this man, joy that she was finally welcoming his lovemaking, that she was truly letting go, discovering the sensation of floating happiness that could come from being with the man she loved. It didn't matter that he was a fisherman, or that in a few days' time he'd be gone from her life, or that he would never make room for a woman in his life. Nothing mattered except the feel of his mouth and hands on her body, his skin against hers, his fevered breath in her ear.

"Mike," she heard her own agonized whisper, "love me . . . please. Make love with me."

"Oh, Kimberly!" Mike groaned. Then, with an enormous effort, he threw himself to the side, away from her. On one elbow he leaned and looked down at her, his face indistinct in the half-light. But Kimberly could see pain mixed with the passion in his face. "Don't say that, Kimberly. Don't, please."

"Why . . . why not, Mike?" She could feel the tears spilling down the sides of her face already. Her voice shook. He didn't want her. It had all been a lie; he didn't want her, after all.

"Because you don't mean it, angel," he said, his voice tight with the iron control he was exerting over a mutinous body. "Nothing's changed, Kimberly. I want you just as much as I always have, maybe more. But nothing's changed for you."

"You mean . . ." She swallowed. Because she was a virgin? Because she'd once said—foolishly and mis-leadingly—that she wanted marriage before she'd sleep with a man? He wasn't going to hold her to that!

"I mean that you're not ready for this, Kimberly." He ran one hand through his shaggy dark hair in silent frustration. Damn! To think that she'd ended up in his bed twice now and that this time he'd nearly— He couldn't help it. He was mad about her, mad about the feel of her, the taste of her, mad about the wind-kissed smell of her....

But it was no good. She wasn't coming to him as a lover should, of her own free will. He didn't know how he knew it, but he did. This had something to do with what had happened between them since the morning spent with the killer whales. She'd needed him; he'd comforted her. Making love with her now would be taking advantage of her emotional fragility, of his role as her confessor.

Mike cursed softly to himself. He'd never felt like this about a woman before, and it was driving him crazy being around her, unable to touch her. But he couldn't seem to give her up, either. Why didn't he just take her to the nearest port and wash his hands of her? Why? Why?

"But you . . . you said you wanted to sleep with me." She was truly bewildered. Her throat ached and her voice was barely above a whisper. What had gone so terribly wrong? Her eyes were huge in her pale face as she looked up, accusing him.

"I did. I mean, I do. I just... Damn it, Kimberly! Tell me why you came over here tonight. Why you're in my bed." His voice was fierce and low.

"I changed my mind. I—I wanted you to make love with me, Mike," she said softly. Truth was all she could fall back on.

He swore softly. "Why?" He was going to force it out of her. He was going to make her understand what he knew to be true.

"B-because you wanted me—at least I always thought you did," she stammered. "And I decided I wanted you, too, after all. I realized it was kind of silly of me to pretend that I didn't. When we, uh—'' Was she blushing?

He bent down and kissed her soft lips gently. "Why else, Kimberly?" There was more, he was certain, but if he was wrong and there wasn't, nothing would make him happier than to make her his, right now, by the pale light of the rising moon. It was sheer torture to pretend otherwise.

"And well, I thought since I'd be getting off the boat in a couple of days that, well, you've done an awful lot for me, Mike. You've—''

"You mean you're feeling a little grateful toward me and thought, 'What the hell? Why not let him have what he wants? I'll never see him again.' That what you thought, Kimberly?"

"No!" She tried to raise herself on her elbows, but he kept her pinned to his bed. "No! You make it sound horrible! It's not like that at all! I just—''

"I decided I didn't want to live by the rules I'd always hidden behind, the ones you made such fun of on Lyall Island," she said, her words tumbling out in a rush. "I wanted to make love with you because—'' She couldn't tell him it was because she'd fallen in love with him and wanted him to be the first. "Damn it, Mike, I'm sick of making excuses for myself because I'm a virgin. Do you know—?"

Mike stopped her protest with a kiss, a loving, gentle, delicious kiss that took away her anger before she'd even got started. When he lifted his head to gaze at her in the moonlight, he was laughing softly.

"You little idiot! You don't need to make excuses for being a virgin. That's one of the things I admire about you. You've kept a very precious part of yourself to share someday with the man you love."

He didn't even suspect the truth. She felt a pain like a knife deep in her heart: he didn't love her, not even a little bit.

"I respect you for it." He kissed her nose gently. "It's not something to...to be gotten rid of, like a wart or something. Now..." He looked at her intently, but she stubbornly stared at his shoulder, refusing to meet his eyes. He went on as gently as he could. "Go back to your own bed, Kimberly. Please. Don't tempt me anymore."

She refused to look at him and made no move to leave.

"Kimberly?"

She didn't answer.

"If you don't get out of here, I'm going to have to get out. Understand?"

When she still made no move to leave, he muttered something and rolled over, his whole weight suddenly on top of her. Then he kissed her again hungrily, his lips moving over hers, demanding entry, tasting her like a man who could never get enough of some rare, exotic nectar that only she possessed. Kimberly met his kiss eagerly, then, with a sudden oath, Mike wrenched himself away. "Kimberly! Why are you doing this to me? To us?"

His voice was agonized, and he swung himself off the bunk and dropped catlike to the floor. He strode to the ladder without a backward look, and a few moments later she heard his heavy tread on the deck, pacing back and forth.

Kimberly let the tears flow silently until finally she fell asleep, alone in Mike's bunk.

Mike squinted into the setting sun through the beer that was left in his glass. He could just see Kimberly's

face silhouetted in amber against the sky, her head
turned to the side as she listened to what Marian Lipke
was saying. Was she smiling? He couldn't tell from this
distance. He hadn't seen her smile much today.

Bill, Marian's burly husband, had gone into the
house to get the steaks for the barbecue. Mike grimaced and drained his beer. Then he stretched hugely
and let out a ferocious growl that delighted the Lipke's
two-year-old son, Terry.

"C'mere, Tiger," Mike said, and scooped the boy up
onto his knee. The toddler grabbed at the front of
Mike's red cotton shirt for balance and screamed with
laughter. Mike growled again and buried his face into
the boy's chubby body.

Fair and dark. Night and day. They were both
laughing. Kimberly watched pensively, her face revealing more than she realized.

"Terry misses him," the boy's mother said with a
smile that encompassed the two across the patio table.
"They have a great time together when Mike's not
fishing."

"Oh?" Kimberly hadn't thought about how Mike
would be with children. He obviously had a quick and
natural rapport with them. As he did with everyone, she
thought a little sourly. Marian and Bill had been thrilled
to see them return to Cortes Island unexpectedly this
afternoon, and there had been loud kisses and hugs all
around. Kimberly had felt a little embarrassed to be in-
cluded into what was obviously such an affectionate
homecoming. He had room in his heart for everyone,
it seemed. Everyone except her.

"Yeah," Marian said, giving her a quick grin. Then she added mischievously, "You're a surprise, though. You must be pretty special for Mike to bring you here."

"Special?" Kimberly managed a laugh and shook her head. She didn't want this neighbor of Mike's to know how she felt about him. "'Fraid not. No, he's taking me home on his way to Victoria. This is just an unscheduled stop."

Marian grinned and winked at her. "Maybe so. But he's never brought a woman to Cortes before. We'd just about given up on him. Bill and I have introduced him to every eligible woman we know and no luck. Bill says I should keep out of it." Marian smiled at her. "I'm a matchmaker. I know. But who could help it when Mike would make some woman such a great catch?" Marian laughed again and stood up. She was a pleasant, freckle-faced woman with a long dark ponytail hanging down her back. It was impossible not to like her.

"Want to come in for a minute? I'm going to bring out the salads, then put Tiger over there to bed."

Kimberly helped her hostess carry out the salads and plates, then wandered down to the shore while Mike and Bill talked by the barbecue.

She didn't notice the sharp glance Mike gave her as she left the patio, nor did she hear him as he approached a few minutes later.

From down here she could see the reflections of the setting sun on Mike's house, barely visible through the trees next to the Lipkes'. His house had been a revelation—of a piece with the man. Rough-hewn cedar logs, planed on one side, formed the walls, and the floor was warm with Island-woven rugs over ceramic tiles and wide spruce planks burnished to a honey glow. The massive fireplace in the living room was built of local stone. Mike had built the house himself, with his own hands and the help of a few friends.

Had she expected anything else? The more she found out about him, the more she realized what a rugged individualist he was, cutting his own swath through life, beholden to no one. Of course there could be no room for another person in his life. Had she really been so incredibly naive as to think otherwise?

Kimberly frowned and took a deep, steadying breath. What a fool she'd been last night! What a stupid fool! Mike had let her down as gently as he could, but it was rejection, cold and clear, all the same.

She'd never forget it: the humiliation she'd felt when she'd awoken the next morning to find herself in Mike's bed—alone. The *Mary Bernice* was already under way. How long had they been sailing? He must have slept in her bed or on the deck. She'd driven him from his own bed! Hot tears of humiliation burned her eyes, and she blinked them back.

"Kimberly?" His voice was soft at her elbow, and she looked away from him quickly, blinking furiously. She didn't want him to see her tears ever again. Then she turned to him, a bright, brittle smile on her face.

"Is the barbecue ready?"

"No, not yet."

Kimberly turned away. She looked out over the harbor. If she could help it, he'd never know how much he'd hurt her. She shaded her eyes. "What's the name of that island out there?"

"Marina Island."

"Is there a marina there?"

He laughed, a deep, throaty sound that Kimberly loved to hear. Her heart lifted for a moment. "No. It's named after a woman, actually."

"Sounds interesting." She cast a quick look up at him. She'd seen his studio, walls lined with his own photographs of ancient Indian petroglyphs—rock carvings—and he'd shown her some of the pictures from the history of one of the early coastal tribes he'd been researching for the past two winters. No wonder he was such a storehouse of Indian legend and lore. Somehow Kimberly didn't think even Uncle Harry knew about this side of the legendary Mike Steele.

"This island—Cortes—was named by two of the first Spanish explorers in this area, Galiano and Valdes. Hernando Cortes was the Spaniard who conquered Mexico. The story is that after the battle of San Juan de Ulloa—farther out in the strait are the Ulloa Islands—Cortes took prisoners, among them a beautiful young woman." Mike smiled down at her, then looked out at the lush green island again. "They fell in love and she became his mistress. Galiano and Valdes must have been a couple of romantics because when they saw how this bigger island held a small and rounded one in an arm of land, they named them for Cortes and his mistress, Marina."

Kimberly squinted up at him, the sun in her eyes. "That's a lovely story."

"It is, isn't it?" he said, smiling down at her.

His tawny eyes filled with a warm golden light that she could only describe as tenderness. How could he look at her like that, she thought angrily, after last night?

Just then Bill called them, and they made their way back up the stony beach. Mike lifted his arm once to drape it casually across her shoulders in a friendly gesture, but dropped it immediately when he felt her stiffen before he'd even touched her.

Kimberly was glad the Lipkes had invited them for supper. They were a boisterous pair and kept the conversation moving. She hoped they wouldn't notice her unusual quietness and was glad that she wasn't spending the entire evening alone with Mike. They'd been on the boat together for nearly three weeks now, in each other's company almost every minute. It was time they both saw other people; time she got home and back to the real world.

On the path to Mike's house Kimberly tripped a couple of times and stumbled in the near-darkness. She would have fallen if Mike hadn't quickly grabbed her. But each time she shook him off, refusing his guiding hand. Finally, when she stumbled for a third time, Mike grabbed her, and this time he didn't let her go. He spun her around and pushed her against a massive tree along the path, then put his hands on the rough bark on each side of her to prevent her escape.

"What do you think you're—"

"I'm forcing you to quit playing games with me, Kimberly," he interrupted. "I'm forcing you to listen to me for once. Look, can we call some kind of a truce?"

His voice sounded immeasurably weary, and the icy shards of anger Kimberly had wrapped around her heart ever since she'd awoken alone in his bed suddenly melted away. What was she doing to this man? The man she loved? All he'd ever done was try to help her. What was she doing to herself?

"You're . . . you're right, Mike. I'm sorry for being so . . . so horrible," she said softly, looking up at him in the darkness. Somehow not seeing him made it easier to talk to him like this. "It's just that you, well, you hurt me so much by—"

"Ah, Kimberly," he groaned, enfolding her in his arms. She was unprepared for the raw note of pain in his voice. "I know, I know. It kills me to hurt you like that and I'm sorry I hurt you, angel, but there's just no other way."

He held her tightly against him, and she felt the strong, deep thud of his heart beneath her cheek. Then he held her away from him, and she could feel him trying to meet her eyes in the darkness.

"You know that, Kimberly, don't you?" he asked, his voice low and strained.

"Yes," she whispered finally. "I know there's no other way. I—I'm sorry, Mike."

"So am I! Lord, Kimberly... so am I." And he held her again tightly, so tightly it hurt, then kissed her chastely on the forehead and released her.

Mike sat for a long time in the darkened living room in front of the long windows that overlooked the harbor. A glass of whiskey rested on the table beside him, and from time to time he would stir from his brooding study of the night sky and the moon on the dark water and raise the glass to his lips. Kimberly had gone to bed as soon as they'd arrived, pleading tiredness and looking as pale as the moon on the water below.

He loved her. It was as simple as that. As simple and as hellishly complicated. He'd known it for the truth finally last night when he'd left her to climb up to the open deck, dragging great gulps of clean, pure, cool air into his anguished lungs. It had hit him like a bolt from the brilliant night sky, and it had scared the hell out of him. For the first time in his life Mike had realized he wasn't in charge anymore, that what was happening to him was way beyond his control. He'd fallen in love with this slim, indomitable woman and he'd give anything for it never to have happened.

He thought he knew what love was. There had been little Rosa Sandik all those years ago, although he knew even at the time that he'd never really loved her—it had just been a convenient way to fulfill his family's expectations, back when doing what other people expected mattered to him. That hadn't worked out and he was glad it hadn't—his cousin Sandy had loved her for years, and he and Rosa were made for each other. Then there had been the teacher with the flaming hair in Campbell River he'd taken out for a year or so. Hell— Mike took a long swallow of the fiery golden liquid— that hadn't been love, either. Love wasn't meant for men like him—loners, wanderers, followers of the sea.

He thought of Kimberly's thick silvery hair, the curve of her cheek in the half-light, the taste of her kisses, the eagerness that had driven him half-wild last night. Lord knows why she'd offered herself to him like that! She didn't love him, and misguided gratitude was the last thing he wanted from her. What did he want? A brief, glorious mating? An affair for a week or so and then goodbye? Two equal and consenting adults offering and giving pleasure the way he'd once, stupidly he realized now, thought of satisfying his—and his partner's— needs?

No, it was her love that he wanted; it was love that he wanted to give her. He wanted her forever. He wanted to make her his and keep her and protect her and cherish her and watch her beautiful body swell with his children. He wanted to grow old with her.

Mike grimaced and drained the last of the whiskey from his glass. He'd never had feelings like that for a woman before—never! He got to his feet, his broad shoulders flexing irritably in the half-light, his profile black against the glass, as rugged as the rough-hewn landscape in which he'd chosen to build his home. He leaned against the windowsill and stared out, his knuckles white as he gripped the frame, his face bleak and expressionless.

It was no use. There was nothing he could offer a woman like Kimberly Bowring, even if he was the marrying kind. And he could never ask her to marry him, even if she did care for him a little. After losing her father and brother at sea the way she had, she'd never, ever, marry a fisherman. And who could blame her?

Chapter Nine

The next day Mike left Cortes Island later in the afternoon than he'd intended, and by the time they'd reached Calvert Narrows he was regretting his decision.

Black clouds scudded silently in from the southeast at an alarming rate, and the sea was beginning to heave and swell with the effects of a summer storm still some distance away. Mike reached up and switched on the marine radio to the weather frequency, listened intently to the snarl and squawk in which Kimberly could barely make out one coherent word, then, with an oath, switched it off.

"We're in for a bit of a blow, I'm afraid," he said with a quick sideways glance. A muscle tightened in his jaw for a moment, then his face relaxed as he gave her a rakish grin. "I'll see if I can race her to Gimlet Cove before this breaks. That'll give us a chance to drop anchor and let it blow itself out."

"I'll go below and make sure everything's tied down," Kimberly said as lightly as she could. The prospect of them being caught in a nasty Strait of Georgia storm brought sickening flickers of anxiety. Surely it couldn't be expected to be that bad, or Mike never would have left the island this late! He wouldn't take an unnecessary chance; he was too good a skipper for that.

All the same, she thought with a shiver, Mike looked as if he was enjoying the prospect. His eyes flicked intently between the sky, the compass and the water immediately ahead of the troller as the *Mary Bernice* plowed steadily through the increasing seas. But a grim sort of smile played about his handsome mouth at the same time. This was the challenge that kept men like him tied to the sea: the thrill of pitting their strength and wits against nature and the joy of victory.

Or the despair of defeat, Kimberly thought angrily. Like her father and brother. And her. She was a victim, as well, too burdened by her fears and memory to move ahead and take charge of her life and her career in marine biology. And what about all the women and children these men left behind when victory eluded their grasp? What about them? At least her father and brother had had to fish for a living; they'd known nothing else. Mike didn't need to fish for a livelihood. But then, she remembered, neither had he chosen to allow a woman and children into his life. No one was at risk but himself. Except...

Kimberly sighed, then frowned as she secured the waterproof canvas covers over the bunks. These past few days had been an emotional roller coaster. There had been the high of finally telling Mike about the accident on the *Gulf Runner* and the sweet, sharp joy of realizing she loved him, and there had been the bitter low of his rejection of her the night before last. Somehow, though, she'd get through the next few days—she wasn't descended from sturdy Newfoundland and Norwegian stock for nothing. And then...? Then she'd forget this had ever happened, she thought, gritting her teeth. Other people fell in love and made fools of themselves and got over it, so would she.

A sudden lurch of the troller sent her skidding down the cabin, and she slammed into the table with an impact that almost knocked the breath out of her.

"Ouch!" Kimberly grabbed her hip. She'd have a nasty bruise to show for that. What was happening? She hurried over to the portholes, but all she could see was the angry lash of gray water against the glass and the occasional glimpse of a dark sky as the troller rolled over a wave.

"You all right down there?" Mike shouted.

"F-fine!" Kimberly yelled back, biting her lip and massaging her bruised hip. "I'm okay!"

This looked like more than a bit of a blow! She quickly secured the objects that could be thrown from their places in the cabin to become potentially lethal objects in the tiny, confined space—not to mention a heck of a mess to clean up when the storm was over. She jammed extra articles into the food cupboards to make sure everything was tight. She'd seen what happened when you forgot—cornmeal mixed with baking powder, salt, jam, flour, pancake syrup—you name it—anything that could break and make a mess, would. When she finished, she pulled on a heavy sweater and raced up to the wheelhouse.

Massive seas were breaking over the bow of the *Mary Bernice,* and the troller was bucking and pitching with each swell. The sky had closed in until the angry black clouds almost touched the water, and then the skies had opened. Sheets of rain slashed at the troller and sliced into the sea. Kimberly could barely see out the wheelhouse for the thick gray web of rain on the glass.

"Filthy weather," Mike said with a wolfish grin that made him look even handsomer than usual. He had already pulled on oilskins, and his hair was ruffled from the wind. He looked quickly at her light jeans and sneakers. "Better get your gear on or you're going to get wet."

"What's the forecast?" Kimberly pulled on her oilskins and boots with trembling hands. She could feel the thin, sharp fingers of an incipient panic attack stroking her viscera lightly at first, then grasping her a little more tightly. Her heart was racing and her palms were damp. She swallowed hard. *Dear Lord,* she thought for one panic-stricken moment, *not now! Please, not now.*

Dr. Gilling had told her that her panic attacks were really only a normal response to fear, the fight-or-flight response, where adrenaline spilled into the bloodstream and diverted blood away from the extremities and into the body core. The animal—or the cavewoman or the modern, postfeminist marine biologist—was ready to run like the very wind to escape danger, or fight to the death to defend herself. If injured, the risk of bleeding to death was lessened and the vital organs retained life-sustaining oxygen to the very end. It was nature's way of making sure enough of the tribe survived to reproduce and perpetuate the species. It was all a perfectly normal part of evolutionary survival—in a situation that warranted it.

But in her case it had paralyzed her life because the panic had struck with deadly accuracy and with absolutely no warning at times when there was no physical danger: planning her itinerary for her research project, standing in line at the bank, in a crowded room, in the middle of an open field, shopping for groceries. It had made her gradually avoid those places where she'd felt the panic, and that was the beginning of the end of her freedom. The fear of another attack had poisoned and stifled her entire world, and that was what this couple of weeks aboard a fishing boat had been all about. Dr. Gilling had said she had to face it to beat it.

"Huh?" She looked around dazed in response to a repeated question from Mike.

"I said, looks like we're in for a rough ride." He squinted out into the boiling sea in front of him, and Kimberly pulled on her sou'wester.

"Uh, yeah," she said absently, absorbed as she was for the moment in analyzing her feelings. She'd taken positive steps to deal with the situation, she reminded herself. She'd be warm and dry whatever happened. But she knew the sudden laughter she felt was desperately close to hysteria. She shot a quick, frightened glance at Mike. Would she be any help to him, or would she freeze up as she'd done so many times before?

Just a minute, Kimberly, she said to herself, running her tongue over suddenly dry lips. Think! He knows what you've been through, and you don't have to hide anything now. It's different this time. And this isn't a panic attack; this is panic! She felt a bubble of genuine laughter rise. It was what Dr. Gilling had always said would happen: when faced with real danger, she would know what to do and do it. Kimberly took a deep breath, then another, and gradually felt a calming effect spread over her tense muscles. It was true. Maybe if she—

"You okay?"

Mike's voice was soft with concern, and she flashed him a quick smile. A hysterical female was the last thing he needed on his hands right now. She felt the panic ebb and noted carefully the feeling of strength that gave her. She could beat it. She could! Besides, she had total faith in him. He hadn't gotten his reputation for nothing. And this was just an unexpected summer blow, after all. Mike knew this coast like the back of his hand.

"I—I'm all right, Mike. Thanks." She stepped a little closer to him at the wheel, and he put his left arm around her to give her a quick, hard hug. It warmed her immensely. She wasn't in this alone. Mike was with her and she could depend on him. The *Mary Bernice* was a sturdy, seaworthy vessel, she had the best skipper on the North Coast at her helm, and there was no treacherous hold of fish below that could shift in a heavy sea. What could go wrong?

"It's not far now, Kimberly," Mike said with another quick squeeze before releasing her. "About another ten minutes, I'd say." He reached up to adjust the radio frequency and volume.

"Mayday! Mayday!"

Kimberly could hear the naked fear in the voice over the radio.

"*Mary Bernice*. Steele here. I read you. Come in, come in." Mike's attention swept to the little gray steel machine bolted to one of the wheelhouse struts, every fiber of his being focused, every muscle tensed.

"—Gibbons, *Sandpiper*. I'm taking on water bad...musta hit a deadhead in this—" Static cut off the man's voice for a few seconds, then they heard, "Looks like I'll have to abandon—"

"Where are you, man?" Mike broke in roughly.

"Just off Brockely Point. North a little, I think. I've—" There was a sound of smashing, rending timber over the tinny channel, and Mike swore fiercely.

He swung the wheel to the right and gunned the *Mary B*'s laboring engines. The look on his face was grim, and Kimberly felt her stomach drop with apprehension. What was he going to do?

He spun the dials with one hand, then swore again and turned to Kimberly. "See if you can raise the Coast Guard at Comox. Channel 16."

His urgency lent steadiness to her fingers as she carefully zeroed in on the emergency channel. Mike turned grimly back to the task of guiding the troller through the heaving black sea.

"I've got them now, Mike."

"Good. Comox Coast Guard? This is the *Mary Bernice*." He listened to the squawk, then gave their position, stated the situation calmly and informed the Coast Guard that he was going to attempt the rescue himself. Kimberly felt her heart literally stop in her chest. "Yeah. If you can support me, okay. But you'll never get a chopper down in this. And Gibbons needs help now." Mike listened intently for another moment or two, then said, "Roger. I'll stand by."

Kimberly had no chance to think in the next fifteen minutes. Mike snapped out instructions to her to ready emergency gear—flares, rope, life jackets, first-aid equipment—and she followed his orders blindly, stumbling from one hand hold to another, trying to keep her footing on the sloping, slippery deck. She could taste the salt on her face from the seawater breaking over the bow. All Mike's attention was taken with maneuvering the *Mary Bernice* into position. Instead of letting up, the storm seemed to be worsening.

Then, when she saw the *Sandpiper* finally, the true reality of what was happening hit her. The other boat was jammed up on some rocks about fifty yards off a narrow point of land. The hard, cold light of a mechanically operated lighthouse winked out its signal relentlessly. *Danger-foolish-humans-danger-danger.* Over and over its three longs, two shorts established its position guarding the rocks of the treacherous sea bottom from the men who sailed. The captain of the *Sandpiper* had had no choice. A maverick from a log boom had punctured his hull, and he'd lost control. The *Sandpiper* was on her way to a watery grave off Brockely Point, and she wouldn't be the first to go down there.

Dear God! What was Mike going to do? He couldn't take the *Mary Bernice* any closer, or he'd risk running his own boat up on the rocks. And he couldn't think of taking a twelve-foot dinghy out to search for Gibbons. Not in these seas!

She turned back to the wheelhouse in response to his shout and struggled to open the door against the wind. Finally she did and stood in the wheelhouse out of breath and streaming with water.

"Here, Kimberly, you'll have to take the wheel. I'm going to run the anchor out."

It was risky; there was always the danger that the anchor would drag and sweep them toward the rocks. But the alternative was to have Kimberly stay in the wheelhouse, trying to keep the troller headed into the wind, and he might need her help outside.

Mike pulled on his sou'wester and reached under his oilskin to fasten the beaver tail of the neoprene life jacket he wore under the rain gear. Kimberly froze at the sight. He really meant to go overboard!

"Mike..." Her voice was strangled. But when he looked up inquiringly, she just swallowed and nodded. She moved over to take the wheel from him, grabbing hard with her frozen hands as she felt the sea try to wrestle it away from her. What could she say? That she was desperately afraid of losing him to the sea? That she was terrified that he would disappear over the side of that boat just like her father and brother had and she'd never see him again? That if he died, he'd never know that she had loved him, that she still loved him, would always— Did it matter that he knew, or only that she loved him? What had she read somewhere—that loving meant dying many times before your own death? If that was so, then she'd loved already and too much.

The sea grasped at the rudder again, and she felt its merciless strength run through the wheel. Enraged, she swung her weight against it. The sea wouldn't win this round! Not if Kimberly Bowring could help it. She hung on, teeth clenched, muscles aching until she felt the drag of the anchor as it took hold.

"Good girl! I'll set the second anchor just to make sure she doesn't pull loose." Mike was gone for a few moments and then ducked back into the wheelhouse. "I saw him. I know where he is, Kimberly," he panted, rain streaming down his face and chest. "He's sent up a couple of flares, so he must have seen us, too. I'm going to try to reach him in the dinghy, but you're going to have to back me up here. We'll need to get a line on the—" He stopped finally and looked for a long, anguished moment at her white face, eyes like dark, fractured pools of amethyst.

God! What this must be doing to her—after the *Gulf Runner*. But she must know... She was from a fishing family. She knew the code of the sea. He had to try to rescue the *Sandpiper*'s crew, just as he'd expect to get help from a nearby vessel if he was in trouble. But how could he say that to her?

Silently he held out his arms, and with a tiny, broken cry Kimberly threw herself into them. For a long moment they held each other, and Kimberly felt the tears stream down her face and onto the slick, rubberized coating of Mike's jacket. Her shoulders shook. How could she bear to let him go? But she knew she had to. She couldn't beg him to stay, for her sake, not when a man's life was at stake. She had to let go. She had to trust in Mike's strength and courage and leave the rest in the hands of God.

She pulled back finally and looked up into his face, her own wet with tears of pain and a sort of strange, trembling joy. She could see the pain on his face, the fierce hungry light in his eyes as he gazed down at her.

"Mike?"

"Hmm?"

"I love you. I—I just wanted you to know that before—" With a groan Mike folded her into his arms again, kissed her wet cheeks and eyes, then took her mouth in a kiss of such great tenderness and passion that she cried out, her love for him overflowing. And her grief. He held her to him, murmuring her name over and over, and then he released her and left the wheelhouse in a rush of howling wind. Kimberly leaned against the wall of the wheelhouse for a moment or so, taking in great gasps of air, then pulled her sou'wester down tighter and followed him out.

The next couple of hours were hell. The only positive element—and that was marginal—was that the weather seemed to be letting up. The rain lashed down a little less furiously and the wind howled a little less fiercely, but the sea was as wild as ever and the sky still as dark. Of course, now it was late evening, almost night, and there wouldn't be light until dawn.

Kimberly watched Mike go overboard with a sense almost of horrified fatalism. She knew there was nothing she could do now but follow his instructions and pray. Using the big floodlight, she followed his progress through the waves; her heart stopped every time he disappeared behind a massive swell, only to begin beating again when he reappeared on the far side. She saw the flare that marked the *Sandpiper*'s life raft, and her throat was dry with relief when she saw the two boats finally approach each other.

This was a difficult point. They had no idea whether or not Gibbons had been injured and how much he'd be able to help in his own rescue. Kimberly held her breath as she watched the rendezvous, wishing she could see what was happening. If Mike was unable to transfer Gibbons into his boat, he'd have to try towing him, and that could be a difficult maneuver. Mike had tied a line from the *Mary B* to his dinghy "just in case," he'd told Kimberly. She didn't dare to ask what he'd meant. There was always the danger that the lines could become tangled or snagged.

Then, cold to the bone and heedless of the rain lashing at her face, she held her breath as she saw Mike begin the slow return to the troller. She couldn't make out whether or not there was a second man in Mike's boat.

Gradually, according to his orders, she winched in the line. Too loose and it could snag on the *Sandpiper*'s raft; to tight and it could swamp Mike's boat if a swell lifted the boat and pulled it away from the troller. Finally, though, she could make out the dinghy, nearly back to the side of the troller.

"Throw down a harness!" Mike shouted from the darkness below. "I'm going to have to pull him up."

He must have broken a leg or something, Kimberly thought, reaching for the canvas harness she'd put on deck earlier. She grabbed it and hurried to the side. "Here it is, Mike!" She threw it overboard and it landed in the dinghy. Thank goodness! She hadn't for a moment stopped to think what might have happened if she'd missed.

Mike bent over the man in the bottom of the boat, and a few moments later shouted, "Send down another line, Kimberly."

Again the rope landed safely in the dinghy. The gods are on my side, she thought with a rising sense of optimism. This is going to work! It's really going to work!

Then, quick as lightning, she slipped on the rain-slick deck and slid under the railing of the troller. Her two legs dangled in space for one endless, horrible moment before she managed to hoist herself back to safety. She heard Mike's bellow of rage from below, and the air filled with a series of choice oaths over the roar of the waves.

"Damn it, Kimberly! What the hell are you doing? You're supposed to have a line on."

A line! She'd forgotten. She quickly snapped the line onto her belt that she was supposed to have put on before Mike had even left the troller.

Then Mike was up the ladder with the line attached to the *Sandpiper*'s skipper. Kimberly was nearly sick as she saw the dinghy below swirling and banging against the hull of the troller. The man in it seemed very still.

"Okay, I'm going to attach this to the winch line," Mike said, working very quickly, his hands sure in the darkness. "Then I'm going back down and you're going to have to take this up slowly while I try to support part of his weight."

"Is he okay?"

"I don't know what's wrong with him. Broken leg, I think. Maybe more. But he's alive."

Mike flashed a grin at her in the darkness, and she caught her breath. But there was no time to examine her feelings. Another second and he was over the side again.

Gradually, muscles straining, lower lip gripped tight in her teeth as she concentrated, Kimberly worked the winch that pulled in the two men. Mike shouted to her to stop once or twice, then start again, and finally she saw them reach the top and rushed over to help.

Dave Gibbons was in a bad way. His face was ashen with a big bump rising on his forehead and a nasty gash over one eye. His left leg was twisted at an ugly angle, and Kimberly knew it had been badly fractured. But he was alive, thank God, and so was Mike and so was she, and Kimberly suddenly felt weak with the flood of happiness that swept over her.

"We'd better get him down where it's warm," Mike said, grimacing with the strain of supporting the injured man.

Between the two of them they somehow got him into the cabin. Kimberly turned up the space heater while Mike tended to Gibbons, gently removing his soaked jacket and sweater and easing on a dry shirt of his own. The man was conscious, but just barely.

"Shall I make some tea?" she said, digging through a cupboard to locate the hot water bottles she knew she'd seen somewhere.

"Yeah. Dave could stand a cup and so could I," Mike said, looking up with a quick smile.

Kimberly suddenly felt very shy. Somehow, now that the crisis was over, it seemed very silly of her to have declared her love for him like that. Still, it was something she had had to do. She had no regrets.

Mike's attention was taken by the gruesome job of removing the man's boot from his swollen leg. He had to cut it off with a Bowie knife, and Kimberly blanched when she saw the angry blue swelling that emerged. Mike probed delicately with his large fingers. Gibbons groaned once or twice, but he remained conscious.

"I don't think it's his ankle," Mike said finally, standing. "Might be the tibia just above the ankle. He's got a lot of bruising, though. Must have got a hell of a bang from something."

Mike carefully splinted the injured limb, holding it securely while Kimberly wound the long white bandage around, very aware of Mike's nearness and the tender care with which he treated the injury. His gentleness, so unexpected in such a large, rough-looking man, had always surprised her.

"Somebody say somethin' about a mug-up?" the injured man said weakly, managing a ghost of a smile.

Mike laughed. "If you aren't hurt bad enough to forget about your tea, Dave, you're going to be all right," he said as he covered the man with the big feather duvet and tucked a hot water bottle on each side of his chest. Who knew how long Gibbons had been drenched in that icy sea, and Mike realized that hypothermia could be the real killer in an accident like this.

Kimberly stirred three heaping spoonfuls of sugar into the man's tea, then stirred some in hers and Mike's mugs. Dave Gibbons needed the sugar in his bloodstream after his ordeal. So did they.

"Ugh!" Mike said when he tasted it. He usually drank his tea black. "Sugar *and* milk?"

"Drink it!" Kimberly said sternly, unable to keep the joy she felt at having him safe and secure beside her again from shining in her eyes.

Nothing more was said. Kimberly gave the injured man a couple of painkillers, tucked him in warmly, then gathered up her blankets and sleeping bag and climbed back up to the wheelhouse. Mike had gone up already to inform the Coast Guard of the situation and weigh anchor.

The storm, although it had abated a little, was still far too wild and dangerous to ride out in their exposed position. Mike had decided to head for Gimlet Cove, as planned, before anchoring for the night. Besides, there was the possibility they might drag anchor where they were. And the rocks off Brockely Point weren't any more inviting now than they were in the light of day.

Kimberly peeled off her sweater and boots and lay down on the makeshift bed she'd made for herself on the floor of the wheelhouse. Mike watched her silently, his hands on the polished wheel, the big engines throbbing beneath his feet. He watched her snuggle down into the soft blankets, close her eyes and sigh, and he felt that sigh ripple through his body, too, with the fierce agony of regret.

She loved him. She'd said she loved him when she'd realized what he planned to do. He knew why she'd done it; he'd have done the same. And then she'd let him go, although God knows what it had cost her to do so after what she'd been through. Could he have done that?

Mike stared out into the black, heaving water, picking his course carefully under the navigation lights. A muscle in his jaw tightened. He hadn't known what she'd gone through, *really* gone through, until—

He felt the raw, thick fear again as he saw her teetering, tilting, swinging above him from the deck of the *Mary B,* and he cursed again, deep in his throat, his muscles instantly clenched with outrage and helplessness. He'd thought he'd known fear before, but he'd never felt anything like he had when he saw her hanging there, when he thought she might be swept away from him. Just like that—gone in the random thrust of another wave. Just as her brother and father had been swept away. Just as he might have been, too, before her very eyes.

And she never would have known he loved her. He hadn't had the courage to tell her then and he never could now. But now it didn't matter. They were both safe. Her place was back in Vancouver, far from the North Coast, her fears faced and beaten. And his place was here, where it had always been, aboard the *Mary Bernice.* There was no future—never had been—for them together. He had to find the strength not to encumber her with what he felt, to leave her free to pursue her dreams as he had always been free to pursue his.

Angrily he gripped the wheel and cursed her foolishness at forgetting to put the safety line on and revealing the awesome power she had over his heart. He cursed Dave Gibbons's luck for getting into trouble the way he had, the *Sandpiper* for taking that deadhead on this night of all nights, the log boom operator for losing that maverick log in the first place and, finally, he cursed himself for the first-class fool he'd been to fall in love with Kimberly Bowring.

At last the troller nosed into the snug harbor of Gimlet Cove. Mike set the anchor, cut the engines and went below to check on Gibbons. He was sleeping peacefully, his face a little flushed, but his pulse was strong and his breathing was good.

Mike stood for a moment in the cabin staring at Kimberly's empty bunk. Then, as though he'd made up his mind suddenly, he stripped off his heavy outer sweater, picked up an extra armful of blankets and climbed back up to the wheelhouse.

Tonight, just for one night, he'd sleep with his lady in his arms.

Kimberly awoke slowly, unsure for a moment of where she was. No, it hadn't been a dream—a slow, warm, delicious dream. The deep, strong thud of the heart beneath her cheek was real, and it belonged to Mike Steele. She hadn't dreamed at all—unless sleeping safe in the arms of the man she loved was a dream. But it was true, too.

She opened her eyes cautiously, reluctant to shift lest he'd loosen his hold on her. But he didn't; if anything, he only held her tighter as he moved a little. He was sleeping jammed against the side of the wheelhouse, holding her close, her head on his shoulder, both arms wrapped around her.

Kimberly looked around. Just the first pale fingers of dawn were showing to the east, casting a gray glow inside the wheelhouse. The troller rose and fell slightly with the swell that reached the cove, but the sky showed the pale even gray that promised a blue sky when the sun got higher. Mike's chest was rising evenly and deeply, the rough stubble of a day or two dark on his jaw.

Kimberly smiled and rested against the solid strength of his chest, happiness and peace flooding through her being. To think that she'd thought him incredibly wild and savage when she'd first seen him! The bravest, handsomest, most honest and trustworthy man in the world. She'd been unbelievably lucky to meet a man like him. And to fall in love with him. She knew he didn't love her—he was too honest even to pretend that he did—but it didn't matter anymore. If she had filled the deep loneliness of his spirit even a little on this trip, she was glad. And she knew he liked her; at least they were friends.

The fingers of dawn were lengthening now, turning the inside of the wheelhouse rosy with an overlay of clearest gold. Suddenly Kimberly felt an immense lightness of spirit. It was a moment she'd experienced only once or twice before in her life. Some of it had to do with the full and rich awareness of her love for this fisherman sleeping beside her; some of it had to do with the knowledge that at long last she'd truly faced her fear and won.

Talking to Mike about the tragedy on the *Gulf Runner* had been the beginning. The rediscovery of her own courage among the ashes of her fear during the rescue last night had completed it. She felt like a new woman: euphoric, light, full of joy. And free for the first time in two years. She knew she'd won—finally. She knew she could beat her own fears if she had to, and from now on she would. It was as Mike had once said: you did what you had to—your best. You could do no more. It was a simple code, and a good one. And it was the only rule he'd ever needed to live as he did.

"Kimberly?"

His voice was deep and soft above her. She tilted her head, happiness shining in her eyes. "Yes?"

"You're awake then?"

He was looking down at her, those fierce raptor's eyes, the eyes of an eagle she'd always thought, full of a strange, soft tenderness. If she didn't know better... "Mmm. I wonder how Dave is."

She stretched a little, very conscious now of the length of his body beside her, hip to hip, leg to leg. They were both fully clothed, but somehow it made little difference.

"Mike?" She heard his answering murmur deep in his chest. "I've made up my mind. I'm going to leave with the Coast Guard this morning when they pick up Dave."

He didn't answer for a moment, but his arm had involuntarily tightened at her first words. After a long moment she felt him breathe out slowly, and some of the tension left his body. "You're probably right, Kimberly" was all he said, and he turned toward her, gathering her completely into his arms. "But we've still got a half hour or so. Lie here with me a little longer."

And she did.

Later, when the chopper arrived with the Coast Guard rescue team, Kimberly was all efficiency, packing up her gear quickly and helping Mike get Dave ready for the airlift sling. Then, when they were finally lifting off, she looked down, hot tears blurring her vision. He looked so alone standing there on the deck of the

Mary Bernice. Alone on the limitless sea. Finally he lifted one hand in a silent farewell.

There hadn't even been time to say goodbye.

Chapter Ten

"I'll admit I'm a little surprised by your attitude, Kimberly. Isn't this what you've been after all along?" Dr. Charles LaRoche, the B.C. Aquarium's chief marine biologist, leaned back in his chair and looked inquiringly at her, his mild blue eyes puzzled. Kimberly was his star biologist, and he'd expected her to jump for joy at the news.

"It was...I mean, it is, Charles. Of course it is. It's just..." Kimberly smiled at her boss. "It's a little sudden, that's all." LaRoche had just informed her that the research grant she'd been angling for since undergraduate days had finally come through—funding for a two-year study on the Robson Bight killer whales from a prestigious American oceanography foundation. No strings attached. That, and that the aquarium had already found a replacement for her job, due to start on Friday. This was Tuesday.

"As far as the job goes, we weren't sure when you'd be back from fishing, and Jack was anxious to get a starting date out of us. If I'd known you'd—"

"No, no, Charles! It's great news. Really it is." She smiled a little more brightly, then got up to leave his office. "I'll get right to work updating my field plans and let you know as soon as I've got something organized. I'm thrilled, honest!" With another smile Kimberly let herself out the door and walked down the corridor to the office she shared with another graduate student.

Of course it was wonderful news. It was what she'd wanted ever since she'd started part-time work at the aquarium almost two years ago. Having the funding come through now was perfect; she might even be able to start preliminary work this fall instead of waiting until next summer. And now she wouldn't even have to worry about working out a month's notice while the aquarium looked for a replacement for her.

That, and finding out that her friend Sharon, who'd sublet her apartment for the summer, was keen to take on a new lease if Kimberly would let her, now that she'd found a job and wouldn't be going back to Kelowna....

There were a lot of changes to think about, a lot of changes all at once. The panic attacks had vanished, and she hadn't had a nightmare in a long time... Things couldn't be better. Except that they couldn't be worse, either. A huge black hole loomed painfully in her life, and at the center of that ache was a tall, dark, shaggy-haired fisherman.

Ever since Kimberly had come back to Vancouver ten days before, she'd been half expecting to hear from

Mike. After all, he had said he was going to Victoria, and that meant he was in the neighborhood—relatively, give or take a hundred kilometers. And they had parted as—well, as friends. Hadn't they? But she'd never heard a word, and the searing disappointment she had felt had startled her.

Everything reminded her of Mike and the few weeks they'd spent together—the fishing boats bobbing at anchor at Steveston near her mother's home where she was staying until Sharon either decamped or she found another apartment, the salt smell of the sea that you couldn't escape in Vancouver, the stark, sleek beauty of the captive killer whales she was collecting data on for the aquarium.

Kimberly looked out the special thick glass of the window that separated the killer whale pool from her office. From time to time Naksa, the pregnant female, or Klandu, the big male, would sweep down and seem to peer with one startling bright black eye into the lighted space where she worked. At times they almost seemed to share her emotions and thoughts, and she was aware again of the natural empathy that the big marine animals seemed to have with their little two-legged land-bound cousins.

Kimberly thought again of the morning she'd spent on the hot deck in the sun with Mike, watching the antics of the wild killer whales all around them in the secret bay he'd shown her. She put her head down on the desk and let the memories wash over her. His touch, the warm male scent of his skin so near her, the silky texture of his hair in the sun, the deep timbre of his voice as he spoke... It had been so perfect; it had been a summertime dream.

Kimberly suddenly sat up and took a deep breath. She drew some papers toward her briskly. It *had* been a dream. And that was the thing about dreams—eventually you woke up and got on with living.

That night when she told her mother about Dr. LaRoche's news, she missed the sharp look the older woman gave her. "Aren't you pleased, darling?"

"Of course I am, Ma!" How come everybody was suddenly so interested in how she felt about the whale research?

"It's just that you've been so...so quiet ever since you got back," Marthe Bowring went on. "I wondered if maybe you'd changed your mind over the summer."

Kimberly shook her head. Had she? Of course not. She'd spent a lot of time preparing for this career, and all her years of sweat and perseverance weren't going up in smoke just because she'd had the rotten luck to fall in love with a trollerman.

Next day Kimberly lingered at the whale pool, jotting down notes from time to time, one eye on the behavior of Naksa. She frowned. Why *had* her mother done what she'd done? Marthe Roaldsen had lost her grandfather at sea, and an uncle. And yet she'd married Harvey Bowring, the Newfoundlander transplanted from the East Coast to the West Coast. There had never been any question that Harvey Bowring's life was fishing. And yet her mother had accepted the risk. Why?

And her great-grandmother Roaldsen. Of course, perhaps there had been little choice back then. If you were from a fishing family in a fishing village in a remote fjord in Norway, if you wanted to marry and have children, you had to fall in love with a fisherman.

Kimberly toyed with her pen, her gaze pensive on the elegant movements of the pregnant female. Had they felt the way she did about Mike? Had they loved their men so blindly and so much that nothing mattered except being with them, sharing in their pain and joy and, yes, even their fears. If they'd loved them so much, how could they have let them go off to sea each season, never knowing if they'd return?

Kimberly felt her pulse suddenly strengthen, and she took a deep, shaky breath. Of course they'd loved their men! What else could have made the pain bearable? That was why they'd done what they had—for love. They'd loved their men enough to let them go, just as she'd had to let Mike go to save the captain of the *Sandpiper,* just as Mike had—

Kimberly flushed and felt her heart pound as a sudden thought struck her. Above all, Mike was a man of honor. He wouldn't dream of influencing her in any way, not after he knew she'd barely survived the tragedy of the *Gulf Runner.* Could she have been mistaken about his feelings for her? She swallowed and took a deep breath. She didn't dare to think it, she didn't dare to hope...

But she had to find out. She hurried back to her office to pull her files on her field research and get a quick proposal together for Dr. LaRoche. She was finished here tomorrow, and before she started anything definite on the killer whale project, she had to find Mike. She had to go back to Cortes or wherever he was and find out if she'd been wrong about him, if there was any chance at all....

She knew now why the Bowring women had done what they'd done over countless generations. They'd done it for love, and so would she.

Next day passed in a storm of activity. Kimberly let her boss know she'd be taking off for about ten days to settle some personal business before she started work on the field study. She cleared out her desk and lugged the heavy boxes out to stash in the back seat of her little Honda. She'd have to set up another office somewhere, but for now she'd store these at her mother's house in Steveston.

Once, just as she was making her silent farewell to the magnificent creatures in the whale pool, she'd gotten a prickling sensation, an exquisite awareness at the top of her spine that had made her almost swear that if she turned around at that instant she'd see Mike standing there, leaning casually against one of the arches behind her, smiling and watching her.

But when she'd whirled around, there was no one there. The ache she'd felt at the illusion nearly unnerved her. What if she was wrong? What if this was just another wild-goose chase up to Cortes? Mike had already rejected her initiative once on the *Mary Bernice*. What was to stop it from happening a second time? But Mike had said nothing had changed for her—then. Now it had.

The village where she'd grown up had once been the only commercial area in this part of Richmond. Fields of diked and ditched market gardens and farms on the rich delta soil had given way to the visual blight of suburban development in the past fifteen years. Only pockets of greenery remained and soon, with a burgeoning population to the north in Vancouver, the little that was left would be paved over. Sometimes Kimberly felt the city closing in on her. Mike, with his love of the wind and the open sea, could never live here.

Finally she made the last turn before her mother's modest postwar frame bungalow and came to a stop before the white picket fence. Her mother's Queen Elizabeth roses, old-fashioned and blowsy, bloomed thickly along the fence, and before opening her trunk to pull out one of her boxes, she stopped to inhale deeply of the simple pink sweetness. Ah! Some things, at least, never changed.

She frowned slightly with exertion as she carried the first of the boxes to the front door, then stopped to lean the weight between her hip and the door frame before she reached for the knob.

The door opened wide before her hand touched it, and her hand flew to her mouth. ''Mike!'' In her surprise she nearly dropped the box. With one quick movement he'd taken it from her and set it down inside the doorway.

''Aren't you going to say hello?'' he asked standing straight and smiling down at her.

''Hello!'' She impulsively threw her arms around him and felt her heart soar as he hugged her tightly and swung her around the room. She caught a glimpse of her mother's beaming face near the entrance to the dining room, a flash of Marthe Bowring's best white organdy apron—the one she only got out for special guests—before Mike squeezed her tightly again and then put her down.

''Happy to see me?'' he asked, his voice low and deep, his eyes glowing tawny gold in the afternoon light.

"You know I am," she said softly, her face flushed. Lord, he looked good! Tall and tanned, and it even looked as if he'd gotten a decent haircut somewhere. He had on a plaid flannel shirt, though, and heavy khaki drill pants, just an ounce or two away from working-men's weight. Mike Steele had come to town, but he hadn't left the sea behind.

She reached up to touch his jaw gently, and his eyes darkened. "Looks like you even shaved!" she teased a little shakily. "What's the occasion?"

He loosened his hold a little and he and her mother exchanged a quick glance.

"Er, isn't this a surprise, Kimmie, dear? I'll get the tea on the table. Mike Steele! For heaven's sake. Coho's told me so much about him. And I'm just thrilled to meet him finally. Living legend, indeed!"

Mike grinned down at Kimberly and she grinned back. They could hear her mother's voice as it trailed off toward the kitchen.

Mike still hadn't released her, and it didn't look as if he planned to. Kimberly could hardly breathe, her heart was beating so fast. "Well, what brings you to Steves-ton?" she said as lightly as she could.

"A couple of things," Mike said, the warm gleam of humor in his voice. He patted his shirt pocket and pulled out a piece of paper. "First of all, I haven't paid you off yet."

Her wages! She'd forgotten all about them, thinking he'd pay her when he settled up his accounts at sea-son's end. He tucked the slip of paper into the back pocket of her jeans, his hand lingering over the curve of her hip and lower back and pulling her in closer to him.

"You could have—" she said weakly. "You could have put it in the mail."

"But then I couldn't have done this..." His eyes dropped significantly to her lips, and Kimberly caught her breath. "And this," he growled softly, his eyes locking with hers, "is what I really came for."

He slowly lowered his head to cover her mouth with his, sweet and tender at first until she felt her knees sag with pleasure and leaned her full weight against him, clinging to him, feeling the iron strength of his arms as he held her. This is where she'd wanted to be for as long as she could remember, ever since she'd seen him wild and shaggy that first day on the *Mary Bernice,* if the truth be known.

She parted her lips eagerly to return his kiss, moaning as she felt his deep hunger for her reach into the very depths of her being. It was the sweetest kiss she thought they had ever shared, and she was sorry when he finally lifted his head, his eyes blazing in triumph, his breathing unsteady.

"Just the way I remembered, angel," he whispered huskily. "Just the way I remembered." He held her tightly, his eyes darkening, his voice very low. "And there's one more thing I came for...."

"Oh?"

She looked up at him, a dreamy query in her clear blue eyes, soft with passion for him. Him! He looked at her pale skin, a little of the summer gold already gone, her straight nose, her hair spilling like spun silver over her shoulders and his arm. She was light and he was dark. She was day and he was night. She was Woman and he was Man. They belonged together; they always had.

"I've come to marry you, Kimberly," he said, the low words more a statement than a question. "I've come to take you away with me and live with you forever."

For a long, wordless moment Kimberly looked up at him, her feeling naked in her eyes. He hadn't said he loved her. It didn't matter; she knew he did. The strength of his love was there—in his voice, in his eyes, in the feel of his strong arms around her. Then she nodded, her eyes brimming with tears, and he crushed her to him, her bent head against his chest.

"Thank God!" was all he said, his eyes suspiciously bright for a few seconds, his voice thick with feeling.

For a long, long moment they clung together, then Kimberly drew back a little, struggling to look up at him. "Oh, Mike..." She couldn't go on for a moment, her eyes telling him everything. "I—I love you so much. I'll marry you and I'll go anywhere with you as long as we can be together," she whispered.

"I love you, too, my beautiful Woman-With-The-Shining-Hair. I always will. I promise." Mike kissed her again, his hands molding her to him, stroking her, caressing her, feeling her slenderness against him like quicksilver against stone. He would protect her, love her and cherish her the rest of his life.

He held her tightly for a moment, then bent his head and grinned down at her, his golden eyes alight with love and laughter. "I think I always have, you know. Ever since I pulled you out of the saltchuck the day you arrived at Toby's Landing. I said I'd never hauled anything quite like you out of the sea before, and I guess I never will again."

Kimberly grinned, loving the deep resonance of his laughter as he held her. "I never thought I'd say it, but I guess we've got Uncle Harry to thank, after all."

"Yeah," Mike said, dropping a kiss onto her straight, sun-dappled nose. "And I've already sent him a case of rum with our compliments."

"You have?" She smiled up at him. He must have been pretty certain of his reception today! She had so much to tell him, so much to— "Mike?"

"Hmm?"

"When?"

"When what?"

"When were you thinking we should get married?" She was thinking of her research project and how she'd go about telling him that she'd already made up her mind that risking love and a lifetime with him meant far more than keeping herself safe and secure from the heartbreak of marrying a fisherman. That nothing mattered more than being with him. No matter what she'd thought and said in the past.

"Right now—today. Or tomorrow."

She looked at him in astonishment.

"Next week at the latest. Just time to go over to Victoria and back. I want you to meet my mother. I've made up with my family, thanks to you, angel. You've made me realize how important other people are in my life, how much I'd cut myself off from—family, loving, the importance of showing the people you love just how much you care..."

"Oh, Mike!"

"As a matter of fact, I can hardly wait," he said, grinning when she immediately blushed. "I've already got the license right here in my pocket." He smiled at her surprise, his teeth a flash of perfect white in his dark, handsome face.

"Pretty sure of yourself, weren't you?" she retorted with the impish grin he loved to see.

"Don't forget—fishermen can read the stars, my love," he said, "and I saw this particular piece of fate written there a long time ago."

"You did?"

"Yeah. I just had to work out the details and hope like hell you'd fallen for me like I'd fallen for you." He kissed her on the nose tenderly, and she smiled.

"I finally figured it out, idiot that I am." She looked up inquiringly. "You see, I was stumped on this business about you marrying a fisherman. I knew you never would, nor could I ask you to after what you'd been through."

"But I *am* marrying a fisherman!"

"No, you're not." He silenced her wide-eyed protest with another kiss. "Listen. I don't need to risk my life in all kinds of weather fishing for a living—not now, not when I've got someone to think about besides myself. I've realized that nothing in my life—not even the sea— is more important than the peace of mind of the woman I love. And nothing is more important to me than being with the woman I love." He stopped and looked deep into her eyes. He looked very serious; serious and tender. "After all, you're my real gift from the sea—I pulled you out."

Kimberly swallowed a hard lump in her throat, her mouth tremulous. He could tease all he liked; she knew what this had meant to him. He loved her; he loved her enough to give up his life of fishing for her.

"So, I've decided to convert the *Mary B* into the best, most up-to-date marine research vessel in British Columbia and to go into partnership with the best-looking, smartest, sexiest marine biologist in the country." He grinned down at her. "And that's you, sweetheart. In between whale projects we're going to raise vegetables and babies on Cortes Island. And I'm going to concentrate on my Indian history books, which I've wanted to do for a long time, anyway."

"I can see you've got it all planned out."

"Yeah," he said a little smugly. Then he held out his hand, eyes gleaming. "Is it a deal, partner?"

She laughed out loud. "It's a deal." And hand in hand they went through to the dining room where Marthe Bowring had just brewed the second pot of Earl Gray, the first one having ended up cold. She beamed when she saw their faces.

"You look very happy, darling!" she said, looking as though she hadn't doubted the afternoon's outcome for a moment. She poured her daughter's tea, then pushed a cup and saucer over to Mike, offering him shortbread and tiny sandwiches. He looked too big and too restless to ever have been allowed to handle delicate English china in a tiny, crowded Steveston living room like this, but like everything else he did, he did it with charm and aplomb.

Mike squeezed Kimberly's hand under the table, and she thought she'd never been happier in her life. "The very best, Ma. The very best."

An hour later, when Mike and Kimberly had told Marthe Bowring about their plans for a quick wedding and left her happily in charge of the arrangements, they walked down to the harbor. There, bobbing at anchor among all the other fishing boats, was the *Mary B*.

As they approached the weathered wooden wharf, Mike swung her up into his arms to the appreciative whistles and catcalls of some of the fisherman working on their boats.

"Just what are you doing, Mike Steele?" she whispered fiercely, very aware that they were the center of attention on the harbor.

"I'm carrying you aboard, my darling, just like they do in the movies. Isn't the bridegroom supposed to carry his bride over the threshold?"

"Yes," she said, relaxing and smiling happily up at him, her eyes twinkling, "and I don't suppose it's any use to point out that we're not married yet and this isn't a real threshold and I can't go anywhere with you right now. I don't have anything to wear for one thing."

She made a slight gesture down at her T-shirt and faded jeans, and he followed the gesture with his eyes, lingering appreciatively over her soft curves until she felt her cheeks turn pink. Then she laughed out loud as he ducked his head to carry her into the wheelhouse. He put her down.

"You're right. It's no use at all. And this is the only threshold you're going to get," he said, firing up the troller's engines and backing carefully out of the berth. He gestured down to the cabin. "Don't worry. I've already thrown a few things aboard for you. Your mother packed them." He laughed at her look of surprise. "Besides, where we're going you're not going to be needing too many clothes." She blushed again, and he grinned, negotiating carefully out of the harbor.

"Since we're not getting married until next Saturday, I thought you might want to bend the rules a little. Have the honeymoon first." He gave her a mocking sideways glance, his eyes alight with laughter. "Why not? We'll start our own tradition. You know how I hate following other people's rules."

She laughed up at him then in sheer, free delight, her heart overflowing with love for the tall man beside her, her silvery hair tangling in the breeze from the open wheelhouse windows and whipping across his dark face. He put his arm around her and pulled her close. They were heading for the open sea with the throttle wide open.

Trust Mike Steele, living legend! He never played by anyone's rules but his own. And from now on, nor would she.

*   *   *   *   *

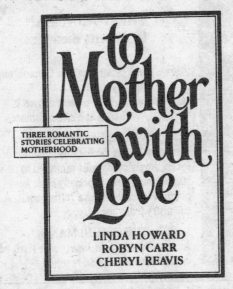

Take 4 bestselling love stories FREE

Plus get a FREE surprise gift!

Bestselling author NORA ROBERTS captures all the romance, adventure, passion and excitement of Silhouette in a special miniseries.

THE CALHOUN WOMEN

Four charming, beautiful and fiercely independent sisters set out on a search for a missing family heirloom—an emerald necklace—and each finds something even more precious... passionate romance.

Look for THE CALHOUN WOMEN miniseries starting in June.

COURTING CATHERINE
Silhouette Romance #801

July
A MAN FOR AMANDA
Silhouette Desire #649

August
FOR THE LOVE OF LILAH
Silhouette Special Edition #685

September
SUZANNA'S SURRENDER
Silhouette Intimate Moments #397

CALWOM-1

 *Silhouette Books®*